DARK ESCAPE

by
Eileen Sheehan

This book is dedicated to incurable romantics who enjoy the paranormal as well.

ONE

As per usual, he was late. This didn't surprise or even annoy Tara. Lateness was a pattern of her father, Ed O'Shea, for as long as she could remember. He focused his archeologist's brain on projects and all else went by the wayside. Ed traveled for work and when he was home his mind rarely joined him, preferring to focus on the job he'd just finished or would soon begin. When her mother died five months earlier, he dove even deeper into his work.

Shortly after her mother's death, the family experienced yet another loss. Her grandmother, Gertrude O'Shea, passed away at the ripe old age of ninety-two. She left stocks, bonds, and other monetary valuables to Tara's father and brother, but she surprised everyone when she left the estate and all its contents to her seventeen-year-old granddaughter. It was accompanied by a letter expressing her desire that Tara do her best to maintain and keep the property in the family. Gertrude even provided Tara with a trust fund to be used for the care and upkeep of the house as well as a modest living allowance that would support her for the rest of her life, providing she lived wisely. Tara knew her grandmother led a comfortable life, but she never imagined the old woman as well off as she proved to be, especially considering the poor condition of the old estate house that she insisted on living in right up to the moment she left this world.

Father and daughter moved into the run down ancestral home the day after Tara graduated from high school and just two months before her eighteenth birthday. They left behind the conveniences of city life, as well as lifelong friends. Of course, it was of little consequence to Ed, but Tara immediately felt the void. Even so, she'd made a solemn vow to carry out her grandmother's wishes to live in and maintain the ancestral abode and she planned on doing just that. With a little elbow grease and a lot of determination, she intended to bring things back to their original glory.

The sun glistened off the morning dew coating the roof top as she surveyed the repair work that was immediately done upon moving in. It looked almost too pristine in comparison to the weathered exterior crying out for paint, and the random spots where the wood along the awnings threatened to crumble to the touch. There were several broken windows. Those that weren't, looked crammed into the wall at an angle, but the structure itself was still solid and sound.

Her chestnut mare's shrill whinny caught her attention. She whirled around just in time to move out of the way of the racing beauty. It brought to mind the need to put fence repairs at the top of her ever growing maintenance list.

Sugar pranced proudly around her. Having been moved from the confines of a rigidly run boarding stable to the free and easy-going environment of a country estate brought surprising vigor to Tara's equine friend. Tara could never get enough of watching her mare's powerful muscles flex beneath her flesh as they met the demands placed on them. It was a sight to behold.

She reached up to pat Sugar's muzzle as the mare gently shoved her owner off into the direction of the barn. Sugar knew that, if she didn't prompt Tara out of her daze, there would be no breakfast. Tara's mind had a way of wandering for periods of time, with little recall of what occurred during the time passed. The clever mare quickly discovered this and stayed persistent in her efforts to regain Tara's attention; especially now that she couldn't rely on stable help to step in when her mistress stepped out.

Tara slapped her forehead as she remembered Sugar's needs and shouted to her father that she'd be back as soon as she'd fed her mare. Ed popped his head out of the window of the second story den and bellowed for her to take her time, since he'd switched his flight to one an hour later. She shook her head, once again accepting his negligence in telling her this bit of information as part of his eccentric persona. He may be scattered and absent minded in matters he found mundane, but he'd made an effort to come home for short visits more than she could remember while growing up. She was just happy to have him around in any way, shape or form.

The odor of fresh horse manure assaulted her nostrils as she entered the old barn. The far corner was made to accommodate Sugar, but the major portion of the barn was still in dire need of cleaning and renovating.

Tara squealed, jumped back, and shuddered as a mouse scurried across her feet. Sugar never flinched.

Instead, the steadfast mare impatiently nudged her feed bucket to bring Tara back to priorities such as breakfast.

Tara's body trembled. She had an unexplainable fear of mice and snakes and couldn't control her reactions whenever she spotted one. As her heart struggled to regain a steady beat, she scooped grain into Sugar's feed bucket.

A flash caught the corner of her eye and chills covered her body. This was no mouse or snake; of that she was certain. She looked around to find nothing there.

"Again," she moaned out loud. "I'm so tired of this, when will it end?"

Tara saw flashes through the corner of her eye most of her life. Mice and snakes may unnerve her, but the flashes and chills were little more than an annoyance. She returned to the task of feeding her mare and then raced back to the house. Her father postponed the flight by only an hour. They needed to get moving if he wanted to make the it to the airport on time.

****

A tall girl of Irish descent, Tara's long, firelight curls hugged her face and fell well below her shoulders in wild abandonment. Her finely muscled frame afforded her the strength to accomplish daunting tasks that most women would buckle under. Yet, for all her strength and power, she retained an air of femininity that brought boys flocking. Hers was the type of personality that people gravitated to. Those who didn't were generally the controlling types who were frustrated by her 'live and let live' philosophy.

Mitchell Woodbourne was one of those control freaks. She'd dated him for two years before he went off to college. She discovered his true colors shortly after he started school, when her surprise visit found find him behind closed doors with a co-ed. Although her first inclination was to tear at the sneering girl's smug face, she managed to retain her dignity and storm from the room with only the slamming of the door expressing her feelings. Mitch later tried to control the situation by demanding Tara realize an open relationship while in college would remove curiosity and he'd be more likely to be faithful when they married; which he was certain they'd inevitably do. She rejected the idea and suggested he go bungee jumping without the bungee.

She thought they had something special and he'd wait for her to reach a suitable age to propose marriage. In a way, she supposed his ridiculous request for freedom dating -while expecting her to sit quietly at home and wait for him- was a clear indication of what marriage to him would be like. She missed his passionate kisses and snuggling into his thick, strong arms while watching an old movie, but she could never consent to his terms.

Her cell phone rang. It was Mitch.

She entered the house in search of her father while she held her stomach with one hand and the phone to her ear with the other. She found her conversations with Mitch more and more unsettling as time went by.

Although his calls were coming farther and farther apart, they were still coming. She needed him to stop bothering her, yet she continued to answer the calls. If she had a brain in her head, she'd ignore them.

Taking a deep breath in resignation, her voice was flat as she said, "Hello Mitch."

"I see your cell phone works out there in no man's land. What other modern amenities might I find? A sink? A toilet? Running water?" Mitch said in a tone that was undeniably sarcastic.

Born and raised in a big city, he couldn't understand Tara's reasoning for living in the old, rundown estate instead of selling it and investing the money into a quality life in the hub of the city.

"Okay," she sighed, "You got your dig in for the day. What's up?" she continued.

"I was thinking about the great time we had last year in the mountains. Do you remember?" he asked in a lusty murmur.

Her body reacted to his sultry coaxing while her mind scolded that she should have known better than to answer his call. His obsession with getting her back was merely because she'd ended the relationship. Of course she remembered. She often thought back on her times with Mitch, especially now that she lived in such isolation. It was time to move on and make new memories.

Did this conversation have a point?

She was just about to ask when he broke the silence, "Hello? Tara? Are you there?"

"What's your point?" she asked in a tone that was colder than she intended.

"Chill," he said defensively. "I just thought it might be nice to take another trip back there. Just you and me, like old days. Dennis can come, if you insist."

She stood at the foot of the stairs and craned her neck

for signs of her father's progression toward leaving. An involuntarily shiver consumed one side of her body as an ice-cold breeze swept past. She glanced around in time to catch the curtains flowing in the living room, even though the windows and doors were tightly closed. She found it odd how her right side was chilled while her left side felt warm and relaxed and made a mental note to check the windows for proper insulation before winter set in.

"I'm able to enjoy the beautiful country side right here," she replied with strained civility, "but you go ahead. It will do you good."

Her side was getting colder to the point of almost hurting. Where was that cold coming from?

"Well," Mitch gave an agitated sigh, "I'll be the judge of how beautiful your countryside is soon enough. Even though you haven't paid me the courtesy of an invitation, Dennis invited me for the weekend. We can continue this conversation when I get there."

It felt like her stomach twisted on its side as Mitch's words assaulted her ears. He sounded like a cat baiting his mouse. She should have known better than to encourage a friendship between her brother and Mitch.

She couldn't expect Dennis to stop the friendship just because she broke up with him. It was true the estate belonged to her, but she'd never even think of lording that over him in any way. She'd invited Dennis to move in with her and their father, but he'd opted to remain in the city to be close to his job but visited on weekends to check in on them and help with any repairs he could.

Even though she encouraged and expected Dennis to treat the estate like it was his own, she and her older brother were going to have to have a serious talk. Boundaries needed to be set.

"Where are you staying?" she blurted.

"With eight bedrooms at your disposal, you'd make me stay in a motel out there in Deliverance?" he asked.

There was a chuckle in the undertone of his voice. He knew he'd won and savored every minute of her irritation.

The cold reached the point of unbearable. She wheeled around for a sweeping view of her surroundings. It was summer, yet this felt like winter.

As her dark green eyes landed on the source of the draft, she stood motionless. Her lids didn't even flutter as she stared into the pale green eyes of an older man dressed in an outdated flannel shirt and wool pants. He was scowling, yet she didn't feel frightened. Maybe it was because she was just that annoyed with him, but she sensed the scowl was meant for Mitch.

When she finally managed a blink, the old man disappeared. As did the cold.

"I have to go. Stay wherever," she snipped as she jammed her cell phone into her back pocket.

What just happened? Who was that man and where did he come from? Better yet, where did he go? Her mind raced.

"Dad, are you ready?" she called a little shakily. "The plane won't wait!"

Her legs were wobbly as she frantically checked the windows and locks while continuing to call out reasons for her father to hurry. She opened closet doors and pounded on their walls, listening for a hollow sound. Sometimes these old houses had hidden rooms. Maybe this man lived in one.

When she and her father were finally on the road heading to the airport, she almost said something to him about the old man, but decided against it. She saw no benefit in worrying him when he'd be half way around the world and unable to do anything to help her.

The remainder of her day was spent searching for the intruder. He probably left while she was away, but, just to be safe and to make sure he wasn't an unwelcome squatter, she searched the house and out buildings thoroughly.

It was dusk before her search was interrupted by Dennis' Cherokee bouncing down the long, sparsely graveled drive with Mitch loudly cursing his indignation through the open window.

Sugar raced to greet them. The setting sun bounced shadows off the mare's powerful muscles as she worked them proudly. She was a sight to behold. Dennis smiled affectionately. He enjoyed the beauty of this magnificent beast. Leaping from the jeep as soon as he'd reached the parking area, he stroked her neck while she pushed him off balance with her nose. Laughingly, he put a little more swing behind his stokes, as if understanding her commands completely. He often joked that she was half human.

Mitch got out of the vehicle cautiously. He wasn't fond of animals, particularly ones that were larger than he was. Whoever heard of a horse that wandered free like a dog? This was one of the little quirks about Tara that drove Mitch crazy. She insisted on treating her animals like they were people. He was about to make a sarcastic remark about just that when he saw her stepping off the front porch.

"Dennis!" She called as she waved enthusiastically.

Mitch scowled as he watched her approach. When he was away from Tara, he held nothing but sweet thoughts for her, but, when he was in her presence, he couldn't hold down his hostility over her rejection. It was a vicious cycle.

Dennis looked at Mitch's scowl and said in a friendly, but authoritative manner, "Let's try our best to get along this weekend."

Tara let out a long groan as she reached them and joined her brother in stroking Sugar's neck.

"Oh no, I'm so sorry! I can't believe this!" she lamented.

"What?" Dennis asked smugly.

"I got involved with something this morning and I don't know where the time went. I never made it to town like I'd planned. I have zip for dinner. How could I be so stupid?" She tapped her head with the palm of her hand and added, "I'm sorry."

Accustomed to his sister's tendency for being preoccupied with projects, Dennis came prepared. He winked at Mitch as he reached into the back seat of the Cherokee and produced Chinese takeout. Holding it high, he smiled with pride. At that moment, Sugar whinnied to remind them she came first. A very grateful Tara suggested her brother and ex-boyfriend to go to the house while she followed Sugar to the barn, assuring them she wouldn't be long.

As the men entered the old estate house, a bitter cold swept over Mitch that permeated his bones.

"Did you feel that?" Mitch asked.

"Feel what?" Dennis replied.

"That...cold," Mitch said.

"It's practically ninety degrees, man," Dennis said. "Are you sick?"

"I never felt better," Mitch mused as he checked the grand foyer for the source of the draft.

He found nothing.

****

Mitch worked the stiffness out of his body. That cold had plagued him all through the night. The summer coverings on his bed did nothing to keep it from disrupting his sleep. He spent most of the night longing for a thick quilt or down comforter. Scowling, he joined Tara and Dennis who were already enjoying breakfast.

The sun shining through the French doors of the breakfast nook brought out the charm of the old estate home. Tara was restoring the house to its original look.

She discovered a method of repairing and cleaning the wallpaper from a "how to" show on public access television and beamed proudly at her handiwork as Mitch surveyed the surroundings. Knowing he wasn't a fan of old, she doubted he'd appreciate her efforts or see the value in the restored rooms, but she let her pride flow anyway.

"There's coffee," Tara announced brightly, "and some

croissants with butter and jam. If you want anything else, help yourself."

She watched Mitch strut toward the kitchen. His thick muscles strained against his shirt. Although they hinted of an attempt to bring order to them, his unruly curls could stand a good combing. His pants were crisply creased and his Armani shirt gleamed of newness. He was a stark contrast to the old house with its faded wallpaper and worn wooden floors.

When Tara returned, he was washing the last of his croissant down with the remains in his coffee mug.

"I'm taking a quick walk outside," Mitch announced. "Does anybody want to join me?"

Brother and sister replied simultaneously with, "I will."

The two winked at each other, gave a quick chuckle, and followed Mitch outside.

Tara walked contentedly behind the two young men while observing the differences between them. Her brother and Mitch were both four years her senior, but that's where the similarity ended. Mitch had dark hair and a large frame with a thick barrel chest and brawny arms. Dennis shared the O'Shea green eyes and reddish blond hair. He was a few inches taller than Mitch with a lean, well defined and developed muscular frame.

The trio decided to investigate the old logging trail up the west side of the wooded hillside. Tara grew up curious to explore it, but her grandmother held firm with her warnings about the perils that awaited anyone who ventured up that path. Although she felt her grandmother a little dramatic, she was still wary about venturing it alone. If there was really peril from an abundance of lifeless trees and sliding boulders, it was irresponsible not to travel in company in case of an injury. So, she'd waited for companions before entering the forbidden territory.

The morning sun barely penetrated the canopy of the trees that coupled overhead along the path. Nature's debris covered the ground that was slick from the morning dew. The smell of earthy decay rose up as Tara's feet sunk into soft layers of rich compost created from fallen leaves and branches. Deer droppings lined the path, giving evidence of their morning and evening march to graze in the field near the woods.

Loud crunching sounded behind her and she smiled at the sight of her mare casually following them. The animal was such good company in the isolation of her new home that Tara sometimes had to remind herself that Sugar wasn't human.

Noticing Sugar was fully tacked, she scowled. She'd saddled her mare for an early morning ride just as Dennis called out for breakfast. She'd fully intended to return for that ride, so she didn't remove the tack. Mitch's offer to walk pushed that ride right out of her mind. Her scattered thinking had increased since she moved to the country and she feared her father's inability to focus was hereditary. She promised herself she'd make sure to remove the tack as soon as their walk ended.

As they approached a small clearing, Dennis pointed out a wooden structure resembling a tiny house. As they got closer, they recognized it as an old well house. Excited and filled with anticipation, she skipped ahead with Sugar close at her heels.

The amount of visible decay to the structure and the plant life that almost consumed it, warned Dennis that the abandoned well might not be safe.

"Be careful!" he called out. "You don't know how sound that thing is and there's no telling what you're stepping on."

Before Dennis finished his warning, a loud crack echoed off the hillside. The ground opened up and scooped Tara into its folds. The only sign of her having been there was the small patch of torn shirt that caught on the wood as she fell through. Sugar reared, squealed, and backed safely away.

Dennis raced toward the gaping hole that swallowed his sister while Mitch froze in his tracks.

Dennis plunged forward on his belly to the edge of the

opening.

"Tara! I can't see her! I can't see her!" he shouted as he turned frantically to Mitch. "Run and call for help! Call 911! Call 911!"

Sugar would have been hard pressed to keep up with Mitch as he pushed his sculpted body into action while Dennis flattened his body on the ground and stuck his head as far into the darkness as he could.

Tara heard the commotion above her, but couldn't move or call out. She felt light, as if floating. She observed Mitch intently as he sprang into action. Memories of their time together flashed before her. She remembered how shy she was when they met and he asked her to the movies for their first date. She remembered how timid and wonderful their first kiss was and how passionate they became as time went on. She remembered how she thought she loved him and no other man could ever measure up to him. Sadness swept over her. She missed him. She longed for his familiar touch and passionate kisses. Then came the memory of walking into his dorm room to find him making love to a co-ed. Her longing for him disappeared as quickly as it came and she once again remembered why they were no longer a couple.

The next thing she knew, she was standing next to Sugar and her attention was directed toward her brother. Dennis struggled to see her within the bowels of the abandoned well. She reached for him and was shocked when her hand passed right through his back.

"You're out of your body. You must return now," said a voice in her head that wasn't her own.

Tara gasped. Did Sugar just speak to her?

She eyed the mare and asked, "Did you say something?"

Sugar blinked a few times and shook her head vigorously.

"If you do not return now you may never be able to. You must go now," she heard the strange voice in her head say in a commanding tone.

Suddenly bright flecks the colors of the rainbow flew about. It resembled driving through an intense snow storm, except the snow was colored. Pain shot throughout Tara's rib cage as she gasped for air. A small cry escaped her lips.

"Tara, are you okay?" Dennis called as he cautiously stretched his torso further over the edge of the hole.

He hoped the well was shallow enough to reach down for her. To his dismay, a loud crack shot out beneath him and he was forced to scoot back to safety.

At that point Sugar was behind Dennis, pushing his back with her nose and working her hoofs into the ground. He looked over his shoulder at her and she threw her head toward the rope fastened on the side of the saddle. He sat like a helpless child on the ground. The stress of the situation made him unable to think clearly. Sugar whinnied and tossed her head more aggressively.

Dennis finally got the message and pulled himself together. He stood up and reached for the rope. Tying one end around his waist, he secured the other end to the saddle horn. The mare had no training for what he was about to ask of her and he prayed for help from above while he fought back panic and he buried his face in her strong neck.

The mare impatiently worked the ground and tossed her head, as if to say, 'get on with it'. Dennis took a deep breath and slowly felt his way down into the depths of the well. The jagged edges made an easy grip for him as he inched his way deeper into the bowels of black.

It was dark, foul smelling, and full of decay.

A soft warm breeze floated past him, carrying with it the sweet scent of honeysuckle. The refreshing difference provided a boost of energy and optimism as he preceded downward, calling for Tara as he did.

"Help," Tara moaned.

The pain in her chest prevented her from drawing enough air into her lungs to produce much more than a whisper. She could only hope her brother could hear her. The rank smell made her stomach queasy. She moved her hand and it nudged the remains of an unfortunate raccoon. Shuddering with repulsion when she realized what she'd touched, she quickly pulled back her hand.

When Dennis finally reached her, he growled with disgust as he kicked the decaying animal remains aside and knelt down to inspect the damage. She looked frail and lifeless.

He cradled her head and whispered gently, "I'm here. I'll get you out."

Dennis dug into the recesses of his mind for the method of tying the rescue noose he'd learned while in boy scouts. Panic muddled his focus. He forced himself to calm down. When he finally managed, his hands moved as if they had a life of their own.

He secured his sister with the rope -wincing with each cry that escaped her pale lips- and then commanded Sugar to back up. To his surprise, Sugar steadily worked the rope. He had little left to do except cradle her head and hold on tight as they were slowly pulled to the top. If he hadn't known better, he'd have thought they were being rescued by several draft horses.

The sound of his Cherokee barreling up the path was clear as Sugar continued to pull Dennis and Tara to safety. Leaves and mud flew as the vehicle slid to a quick stop. Mitch hopped out and rushed to help with the final stages of the pull.

As the two came into sight, Mitch reached forward and grasped Tara beneath the arms. He lifted her like she weighed that of a tiny child, lowered her gently to the ground, and then turned to assist Dennis with equal ease.

Beads of sweat coated Mitch's face and neck. His breathing was labored. He hadn't stopped to think about what he'd done. He'd just kicked his body into gear and did what he needed to do. Now, as he rested for the first time since the nightmare began, his muscles complained about the strain he'd put on them. He'd heard of situations where people developed super human strength and were able to lift things like cars in a crisis. He now knew the stories were true. He fell back onto the soft moist ground, ignoring the tiny leaves and twigs that pierced his flesh through his designer clothes.

Dennis inspected Tara. Her face was pale and her lips were a faint purple-blue.

"Did you call for help?" He barked to Mitch, a little more gruffly than intended.

Mitch chose to let Dennis' tone of voice slide.

"They should be here any minute," he said through heavy breathing. "Should we take her to the house? I don't know. What do you do in a situation like this? Should we move her or wait?"

"How hard was it to get the jeep up here?" Dennis asked as he looked anxiously at the mucky path.

"I slid a lot," Mitch said. He shook his head and added, "They'd be foolish to try getting an ambulance up that path."

Dennis shook his head. He knew moving Tara, without an understanding of any injury she may have obtained during her fall, could worsen the situation, but he didn't know what else to do.

"I don't want to risk them getting stuck. Help me get her into the back of the jeep. Lower the back seat, will you?" Dennis asked; making a conscious effort to keep his voice less aggressive.

Mitch rose to his feet. He no longer had speed or power in his movements. It felt like lead was pumping through his veins. Each step forward was a struggle.

Dennis pulled a blanket from the back of the Jeep and spread it onto the ground near Tara.

"We can carry her in this," Dennis suggested as he shook out the blanket and spread it next to her. "Maybe it will help balance her weight and not jog her as much. You take that side."

They eased Tara onto the blanket and wrapped her

tightly. Dennis grabbed Mitch by the wrist in a firm hold. His expression of gratitude and friendship when their eyes met caused a lump to form in Mitch's throat.

Clearing his throat, Mitch said, "Come on buddy... on the count of three".

TWO

Tara snuggled deep into the mound of pillows piled beneath her back to keep her torso elevated. She was released from the hospital that morning and it was wonderful to be home. Her mother's sister, Eva, gripped a bed tray as she entered the room. She'd traveled from South Carolina as soon as she learned of the accident.

Tara's stomach responded with a loud rumble to the aroma of the homemade chicken soup and freshly baked rolls on the tray Eva balanced with care. She giggled as she watched her aunt struggle with the heavily laden tray.

"You're spilling my salvation," Tara teased. "You never were good with carrying trays. It's no wonder they fired you from that waitress job."

"Pick on me and I'll send you back to the hospital," Eva teased back. Her big doe-like eyes twinkled with delight.

"No, anything but that," Tara feigned despair.

Eva gently placed the bed tray across her niece's lap and then busied herself by patting more fluff into her pillows to provide more support for her back. Tara watched her fondly as she bustled about the room opening windows, shifting draperies, and picking up loose clothing.

"I felt a little breeze in my room last night, even though the windows were closed. It's warm now, but I think you should tend to it before the winter months come," Eva said. She reached forward and patted Tara's knee, "We'll focus on that when you're well again. I need to go fix dinner. Dennis is like a bear if he doesn't have a full belly."

Tara knew Dennis would be anything but a bear if

there was no dinner, but feeling needed like that seemed to comfort her childless aunt; so she said nothing. A successful writer, Eva often imposed the traits of her characters onto her companions. The siblings lovingly tolerated Eva's eccentricities -that apparently ran on both sides of the family in one form or another.

"How's your novel coming?" Tara asked quietly between spoonfuls of the delicious soup. "What's it about? I can't remember."

"The novel's coming along fine," Eva replied proudly. "In fact, it's almost done. You can't remember what it's about because I didn't tell you, but nice try."

Tara heaved an impatient sigh and dove into her fare with exaggerated gusto. She hated secrets. Eva consistently refused to divulge the theme of her novels until they were in print. Her way of making it up to her niece and nephew was to present them with autographed first editions. Tara couldn't understand where Eva came from with her superstitions. Just once she'd like to be able to know the plot before the world did.

"If you need anything before I get back, I placed a small bell on the night stand. It's cute, right?" Eva chuckled as she finished loading her arms with laundry and headed for the door.

Her chuckling shifted to sweet singing as she made her way down the once majestic stairway with her bundle.

Tara was dipping the last of the rolls as a sponge to absorb the remains of the chicken broth when she felt that all too familiar cold on the right side of her body. When she turned toward the window she caught a flash in the corner of her eye. She sat still, barely breathing. The same man who appeared the day before her accident was standing at the foot of her bed. He stood completely still, watching her; simply watching her.

"Who are you?" Tara said, breaking the silence.

The old man stood silent and motionless.

"What do you want?" she persisted. "Where did you

come from?"

The harshness of Tara's whisper hinted at the panic she felt as the man continued to stare. Who was he? How did he get into her room? Was he a thief, a rapist, a murderer? She scrambled for the little bell on the night stand and swung it wildly. When she checked to see the man's response, he was gone.

"What's the matter?" Eva asked as she rushed breathlessly into the room.

The way the bell rang, she wasn't sure what to expect when she entered. The sight of her niece's pale, frightened expression stopped her in her tracks. She followed Tara's stare and saw the curtains flowing even though the windows were closed. She could see nothing except that her niece's room needed weather proofing like the rest of the house.

"I... I thought I saw someone," Tara stammered.

"Where?" Eva asked as she walked around the room looking behind fabrics, into closets, and under the bed.

"There's no one here and the hall was empty."

"It must be the medicine," Tara moaned.

"Get some rest," Eva said as she patted Tara's hand and tucked the covers around her.

Seeing her niece so obviously distraught, Eva made a mental note to remind her nephew to see that the entire house was weatherproofed in time for winter, before moving to Tara's side and wrapping her in her arms.

****

Dennis approached his aunt from behind and placed his hands on her shoulders as she quietly rocked in the rocking chair on the patio. They remained as if suspended in time, neither one willing to speak and break the silence that permeated the air while they reveled in the beauty of the fiery orange ball that majestically inched its way behind the trees.

Dennis often marveled at such wonders of nature.

When he was a small child, he'd sit in Eva's lap and study the stars. Eva used to point out the constellations and sometimes tell stories about the gods and goddesses associated with them.

"Are you up for some wine," Dennis asked as he rested his cheek against her cheek.

She nodded.

"I'll get it," he said as he placed a quick kiss on her cheek. "If you're a good girl, I'll let you tell me all about the stars."

"Oh?" Eva laughed and lovingly patted her nephew's hands. "You're so good to me." She rose and made her way into the house where the wine rack rested in the corner of the dining room. "Let's see what kind of stock my dear brother-in-law maintains."

Dennis followed her.

"I said I'd get it. You can't sit still, can you?" he said with a teasing sigh.

She grinned sheepishly and shrugged while she continued to select a bottle of wine from the portable bar. The selection was limited, but good.

While her aunt and brother enjoyed a quiet evening of star watching and wine, Tara fell into a deep sleep; taking with her that disturbed feeling that clung tight since the man appeared in her room.

She tossed uncomfortably as she relived the experience of falling into the well. For the first time since the accident, she recalled the way she was able to communicate with her mare. She relived the piercing pain of re-entering her body and bolted up in bed, trembling as she gasped for air.

The room was abnormally dark and she could barely see her hand in front of her. Eva, thinking Tara needed as much undisturbed rest as possible, took great pains to tightly secure the drapes over the windows to prevent any evening air from coming in through the cracks and help muffle outside noises.

A glowing ball slowly manifested in the corner of the

room. Tara covered her mouth while she watched a robed figure step regally out of the ball. It reminded her of the science fiction movies where people traveled through space and slowly re-materialize. The figure glowed in such a way that she expected to feel heat radiating from him and was surprised when she didn't. Suspecting she was still dreaming, she rubbed her eyes and squeezed them shut in hopes that when she opened them he'd be gone. He wasn't. Try as she may, she was unable to see the face of her mysterious apparition. It was tucked far too deep in the wells of the hood of a rich, blue-grey cloak.

"Hello?" she whispered.

"Greetings. May the grace and peace of the Eternal One be upon you," he said in a tone that caused a soothing calm throughout her entire body.

Then he was gone.

Tara stared while the light faded and the room went dark again. She made a mental note to check the side effects of the medication she took and drifted peacefully off to sleep.

Her body felt weightless. The dark room around her gradually receded and she was floating amidst wisps of clouds. She felt a tug on her shoulders, as if someone was pulling her down. She resisted, briefly, before giving way to the motion. As she drifted downward, her surroundings grew more visible. Beautiful lakes of an indescribable bluish-green glistened while reflecting the shapes and colors from the leaves on the trees. On the water's edge, stood a cloaked man. His cloak glistened with fine strands of gold and silver. They added to, instead of masked, the base color of blue-grey. When he moved, he created a magnificent sight.

The grip on Tara's shoulders loosened and she found herself in a field of flowers of all shapes and colors. Beds of roses without their thorns, coupled with lilacs, lilies, and every flower imaginable stretched into nothingness. Oblivious to whether it was their season or not, they simply coexisted in this massive field that seemed to go on forever. As the flowers gently brushed her bare calves, happiness exceeding anything she'd ever felt before radiated through her. She could remain there forever.

The figure in the cloak stood motionless while she worked her way across the field of radiant colors until she would be able to reach out and touch him, should the desire to do so strike her. This time his face was clearly visible. It was a gentle face; clean and free of facial hair and milky soft in appearance. It bore no wrinkles from age, worry, or anger. His eyes were the deepest blue-green she could remember seeing. They reminded her of the water they stood next to.

He smiled softly, "Greetings. You are most welcome."

His twinkling eyes watched patiently while she drank in the sight of him.

"Who are you?" she asked when she finally found her tongue.

"I have been with you since before this embodiment and I shall be with you while you walk this planet and there-after. We are bonded." He said in words that were a gentle soothing song to her ears. "I am Liam."

As she absorbed the words that floated gently and clearly through her head, Tara realized that Liam's mouth hadn't moved.

"I have been watching closely," Liam continued. "Since you will need assistance soon, I chose to remind you that I am here."

"I have no idea what you're talking about," she murmured.

She marveled at her lack of fear. She actually felt safe and secure. She shook her head. Should she be so complaisant about this? Should she be reveling in this wondrous relaxation when she had no idea who this Liam character was? What did he mean when he said that they were bonded?

She knit her brows together and tension returned. Liam gave a little smile and gently swept his hand close past her face. She felt a slight pressure, but not his touch. Once again joy mixed with peace and tranquility swept over her.

"I am your guardian in spirit," Liam explained. "It is my task to work with you while you are in this growth process. I am honored to assist you in expanding your knowledge of the earth plane, as well as the spiritual plane."

His voice stayed smooth and gentle.

"I'm not sure I understand," she stammered.

She found it difficult to harness the thoughts and form them into sentences.

"In time, you will become strong in your understanding and you will be able to share with others what you have learned," he said. "In the beginning, you will feel tired from our meetings. I assure you this is temporary and you should not be alarmed. No harm will come to you here. You are loved and protected. You may call on my guidance at any time, for I am always near."

Again Tara felt the pull on her body. It was like someone was steering her through space. The beautiful surroundings faded and once more she found herself enveloped in a cloud. She hovered there for a moment before opening her eyes and finding herself snuggled safely in her bed.

Her eyes snapped open and she cautiously checked out her surroundings. Dust speckled streams of morning sun peeked through the cracks of the fabric barrier Eva created the night before. Faint singing of the birds filtered through the glass barrier, bringing a smile to her lips. She stretched in a cat-like manner and rolled over. She wasn't quite ready to give up that feeling of euphoria and come back to reality.

****

The trio lived in harmony for the next two weeks while Tara steadily regained her health. Eva and Dennis dove into some much-needed house repairs. Eva worked diligently each day, while Dennis drove in from the city on the weekends to do what he could. They repaired a large hole in the paddock -where Eva insisted Sugar remain- and finished the paint job that Tara started on the porch.

Tara had a slow and methodical way of working. Eva, on the other hand, was swift and to the point. She completed an easy two months' worth of work for Tara in two weeks.

Eva didn't hear Tara walking up behind her as she eased herself cautiously into the wicker rocker on the patio to enjoy yet another magnificent sunset. Her muscles ached and her movement was noticeably rigid.

"You're hurting," Tara said softly.

"You started me!" Eva exclaimed as she covered her heart with her hand. "I'm sore, but I enjoyed putting around." She let her body sink deeper into the rocker. "I think I'll go home. You're pretty well recovered and I'm behind on my manuscript."

Tara positioned herself on the cool flagstone patio at Eva's feet and laid her head in her aunt's lap. She always hated to see her aunt leave.

"I was too sick to even enjoy your stay," she whined. "Can't you stick around a little longer so we can do a few fun things together? Please?"

"I wish I could, but I took off in such a rush that I left a lot of loose ends. My publisher's asking for the final chapters." Eva stroked Tara's soft locks while she stared absently across the shadowy fields at Sugar, who grazed peacefully. "You'll be fine now," she continued. "I'll be back before you know it. I still plan on making my regular visit. Don't think this is a sub-stitute."

Tara giggled and snuggled her cheek deeper into Eva's lap, like she did when she was a little girl. They stayed -each deep in thought- until the cool fog of the evening forced them to move inside for warmth.

Eva took a long look around at the interior of the charming antique house. It would be quite a beauty once it was restored. She could almost feel the life and hear the laugh-ter of the years gone by. There were marks on the woodwork leading into the laundry room where the growth of children from early years was monitored. The slight curve of the stairway leading up to the second-floor added grace and elegance, while the intricately carved banister boasted style and charm.

It was an unusual country house to be found in the north. It had the style and charm of a southern plantation home. She wasn't aware of such structures on northern farms and estates. It seemed far too grand, even in its run-down condition. She felt as if the wonderful house smiled with gratitude at the work she and Dennis completed. Yes, she'd be back, and would be happy to come.

The next morning, Eva was packed and saying farewell. Tara reluctantly waved as Dennis chauffeured her aunt off in his Jeep Cherokee. Tiny puffs of dust rose from beneath the Jeep's wheels while it disappeared down the drive.

She found the intense silence left behind unnerving. An eerie feeling that came over her as she observed the stillness. Seeking the refuge of companionship, she headed toward her pacing mare, who was clearly not appreciative of the repair work done to contain her in the paddock.

The pungent aroma of the horse's body mingled with the scent of grass and a hint of manure. Tara inhaled deeply, taking in as much of the familiar smells as she could while reveling in the comfort she immediately received for her unsettled nerves. She wanted to erase the gap of time that elapsed between herself and Sugar while recovering from her fall.

Sugar turned her nose deep into her mistress's side. The mild pressure to Tara's ribs brought a twinge of pain and she flinched.

'I see you are not yet recovered.' Sugar's thoughts penetrated their way into Tara's head.

"Not quite, but it's much better" she replied before realizing she'd received a telepathic message from her horse.

It sent her bolting backward and stumbled to the ground.

Confusion enveloped her as she scrambled toward the fence. Her breathing labored and the threat of hyperventilating hovered. The mare watched Tara's reaction briefly before returning her focus to the luscious rich pasture that awaited her.

Regaining a semblance of composure, the startled young woman rose shakily and made her way back to her mare.

"Did you do what I thought you did?" she asked warily.

Sugar steadfastly grazed and reveled in the juiciness of the rich green grass as if deliberately ignoring Tara's question.

"Sugar!" Tara demanded.

Tara was sure Sugar was demonstrating her dissatisfaction at being disturbed, when the mare turned her rump toward her, urinated, and walked away.

Confused and exasperated, Tara returned to the house to lie down until Dennis returned. She'd experienced a firm pressure in the middle of her forehead while communicating with Sugar that transformed into a full-blown headache. Perhaps this was just a hallucination of some type. After all, she'd suffered a terrible shock when she fell and she wasn't quite recovered. Maybe she just overdid things and this was a result of it. Once again she made a mental note to check into her medication.

Tara stopped at the top of the steps leading up to the broad wraparound porch and watched the peacefully grazing mare. There was something familiar about the pressure she felt while communicating with Sugar, but she couldn't quite place it. The brief memory of a glowing robed man came and left just as quickly.

Making her way toward her bedroom, she decided it would be best not to mention her dream or her telepathic hallucinations to Dennis. Some things where better left alone.

THREE

Tara healed and grew stronger as time progressed. She spent her days doing light jobs and keeping contact with Dennis via telephone and computer. With their father overseas, he'd taken on the role of head of family. He'd also gotten annoyingly protective since the accident. It took a while, but he eventually loosed his grip to a tolerable level.

Although the peace and solitude was initially a welcome change from the hustle and bustle of Manhattan, it was wearing thin. Dennis did his best to come on the weekends, but work was demanding and his visits were not as regular as Tara would have liked. She longed for companionship; to have someone to talk to, laugh with, and even fight with. She'd yet to venture into the small village in the heart of the valley five miles east. She was content to explore her new home and ride Sugar to the country store to purchase any of the staples they might need. She decided it was time to break up the monotony by exploring the nearby town.

Wearing a light gingham sundress and a broad rim straw hat, she headed toward the shed meant to house the field equipment, but now garaged her twenty-year-old mustang convertible.

Her face twisted in disgust at the bird droppings that covered the canvas top. She brushed as much of the dried droppings off the car as she could with an old broom and tackled the rest with a water hose while hoping the ammonia in the droppings hadn't damaged the finish; shuddering with revulsion the entire time. There was something about bird droppings she found repulsive, which was odd considering she shoveled horse manure daily.

Satisfied with her work, Tara eased herself into the driver's seat and started down the drive.

Her mare's silken mane and tail flowed as her lean muscles worked to keep up with the convertible on her side of the paddock fence. She reared and squealed as Tara turned onto the macadam road and picked up speed.

Then, with surprising aloofness, she returned to grazing.

Taking one more glimpse at her mare in the rear-view mirror, Tara pondered what it must be like to be a horse.

How quickly and easily they fluctuated between being entertained and bored. She shook her head as memory of telepathically communicating with Sugar flashed through her mind. She touched her forehead lightly to help shake the thoughts free so she could focus more clearly on driving down the unfamiliar road toward an unfamiliar town.

Enormous trees lined the winding and hilly road, giving it a stately air. She longed to feel the full effects of the warm, fresh air coming through her opened window. She decided her top was probably dry enough to lower.

Noticing a narrow dirt road leading off into the trees, she eased her car onto it; making sure that she was far enough away from the main road to avoid any mishaps with cars zooming by.

For the most part, Tara enjoyed driving her retro vehicle, but this was a time when she'd have appreciated the convenience of mechanical automation.

As she stepped out of the car and she felt the familiarity of musty foliage beneath her feet, her thoughts flashed back to her accident. Her body trembled as she peered up at the sky through the trees and remembered looking up into the sky from the depths of decay and rot filled well.

The sound of snapping branches caught her attention. She turned to discover a beautiful deer standing completely still while it watched her warily, poised for flight at a moment's notice. She stilled her body and breathing as quietly as she could while her eyes locked with those of the statuesque creature. To her dismay, their encounter was cut short when she unexpectedly let go a riotous sneeze that sent the deer flying into the depths of the foliage.

She didn't notice the woman approach her while she fussed to set her nose aright until the sun's rays created a shadowy outline of her. As the woman moved to the left, Tara was able to get a clearer view. She was about Tara's height, but doubled her width and triple her age. Flecks of gray topped off her sun kissed auburn hair that was worn in a long straight braid down the middle of her back, almost touching her waist.

"That's a pretty car, lass," The woman said with a distinct Irish brogue that bounced off the trees as she caressed the vehicle. "You're a lucky young woman to be able to drive the likes of this. It's a convertible too. Imagine that. I've never seen the likes of something this lovely in me whole life. Where are ya coming from?" she asked as she grabbed the other side of the canvas top and helped Tara secure it in place.

The enthusiasm of this stranger was infectious.

"I live just up the road," Tara said eagerly. "I moved here in the beginning of summer and I'm only now getting out exploring the area because I had a terrible fall into an old abandoned well and was injured. I converted my utility shed into a garage and the pigeons pooped all over my car, so I had to clean and wash it off and needed to wait for the top to dry before I could put the top down and enjoy the sunshine and warm breezes."

Tara couldn't explain why she felt compelled to babble like that, but it just seemed the natural thing to do.

The woman nodded intently, her clear, but faded green eyes focused on Tara's mouth as if absorbing and digesting each word spoken. Her head shook in rapid agreement and a slight groan of empathy escaped her when Tara reached the part about the pigeon poop all over her car. There was something about her that Tara immediately gravitated to.

"Where are ya fixing to go?" she asked. "In two blinks and a handshake you're in and out of that wee town. I'm headed there myself to do me weekly food shopping. Perhaps ya wouldn't mind me joining ya in this beauty?"

"You're on foot?" Tara asked incredulously.

"I enjoy a good stretch of the legs, but this beauty is calling me to ride with ya," the old woman explained.

"Absolutely," Tara giggled, happy for the company. "I'd be delighted."

"What a grand lilt of a voice ya have there, lass, 'tis music to these old ears," the woman said as she lowered her herself into the passenger's seat. "We're neighbors, ya know. 'Tisn't polite not to socialize, I know, but I keep to meself mostly. I'm Maggie O'Shea."

"What a coincidence. We have the same last name. I'm Tara O'Shea," she said with surprise while studying Maggie's aged face and physique that hinted of strength and power beneath her green tee shirt and loose faded jeans. There was a familiarity about her that she couldn't place, but she was certain it would come to her in time. "Are we ready?"

Maggie, who'd been studying Tara with knit brows as if to remember her as well, took a deep breath, presented a broad smile and said, "Indeed we are."

****

Tara spent the day getting to know the area with Maggie as her guide. The two women where an unlikely looking couple, yet there was something about Maggie that Tara found delightful. She felt an instantaneous trust and security with the woman. They shared stories about themselves, about people they knew, and places they'd been to. They compared likes and dislikes and discussed trusts and distrusts.

To Tara's delight, Maggie had a passion for animals that surpassed her own. On a whim, she invited the old woman back to her house to meet Sugar. It was an invitation Maggie readily accepted. As they approached the driveway, Sugar pranced at the edge of the paddock.

"That's Sugar," Tara smiled broadly as she pointed to the mare with pride.

"She's a fine animal. She's such a strong love for ya. Yes, yes... a strong love indeed." Maggie said as she inspected the mare with her eyes. "She hurt her wither?" she said more than asked and scowled. "Ooooooeeeeee. That must have been painful!"

"Why would you say that?" Tara asked.

Her surprise made her words sharper than she meant for them to sound. She saw no indication in Sugar's manner that would denote an injury anywhere on her body. Because she took such pride in the care she gave her mare, she was a little offended at the concept of an injury slipping past her.

If Maggie noticed the sharpness in Tara's tone, she made no mention of it.

"Stop the car missy and let me get closer to the beauty," Maggie said in a mannerism that was gentle, but firm.

Tara pulled to a stop and they walked to the fence. To her amazement, Sugar immediately went to Maggie; who scratched the mare's head and rubbed her ears with zeal. Sugar's eyes closed as she reveled in the sensation. Maggie stood back and looked directly at the mare. Neither one moved. Finally, the mare tossed her head high in the air and whinnied.

"Where's the gate?" Maggie asked as she craned her head from side to side while searching for the entrance to the paddock. Without waiting for Tara's response, she climbed the freshly whitewashed wooden fence with the ease and grace of a cat, dropped lightly to the other side, and strode up to the mare.

Tara wasn't as graceful. She hitched her sundress up around her thighs to free her legs for climbing. Her open toe sandals left her skin exposed to the weathered wood, necessitating caution against slivers. She hung clumsily over the top rail and stared in wonder at the vision of this strange Irish woman and her lovely mare.

Maggie gazed steadily into Sugar's eyes while neither of them moved. Next, the old woman held her broad hand just above the mare and slowly passed it over the animal's muscular body. She stopped at the whither and turned to Tara.

"'Tis mighty painful here still, lass," she said. "Why did ya say she wasn't hurt? She's plenty sore here. She says she hurt it when she pulled you and your brother out of that big hole ya fell into a while back and it hasn't finished healing. It must've been mighty sore. That's a lot of weight for a horse her size to pull on. Ya sure are lucky to have such love and loyalty from this beauty."

Tara dropped to the ground with a thud. Her knees buckled beneath her and she lost her balance, falling forward like a rag doll beneath the mare's stomach. This brought rolling laughter from Maggie. Her bright eyes watered from the intensity of it. Realizing what a sight she was, Tara joined in. It felt good to laugh.

When their laughter was spent, Tara rolled out from beneath her steadfast mare and asked while she stood and brushed debris from her dress, "How did you know Sugar was hurt?"

"I got the gift, honey. I got the gift, but ya have it too. Here," Maggie said as she reached for Tara's hand, "look at that hand. Can't ya see? Ya heal, lass. You're a seer and a healer. 'Tis easy to see."

Tara was almost overwhelmed with confusion. What was Maggie talking about? She wasn't a healer. She wasn't a seer. Heck, she was barely a woman! What did it mean anyway? She knew what a healer was, but what was a seer? She closed her eyes and placed her fingers to her temples. Her head felt like hammers were let loose inside it. She saw visions of the accident at the well, followed by a fleeting glimpse of the cloaked man from her dreams.

A frustrated groan escaped her lips.

"Are your memories hurting ya?" Maggie asked gently.

"Not to worry, 'tis normal. It'll get easier as ya open up to the flow. Just relax now, Maggie's here. Relax... relax."

Maggie moved closer to Tara and placed a large and weathered hand on the small of her back and the other on her forehead. The roughness of her calluses didn't interfere with the waves of energy that flowed through Tara, leaving a sensation of peace and tranquility in their wake.

Feeling at peace and safe with her new-found friend, Tara opened up to Maggie.

"Sometimes I think I'm going crazy," she began. "I see things, really strange and weird things. I see people who aren't really there! They just show up and then, pouf, they're gone. For crying out loud I even sometimes hear my horse talking."

"Now don't go getting all riled," Maggie said as she removed her hands and straightened her back. "I just got ya relaxed. Nothing's going on here that isn't normal. 'Tis the way of our kind, that's all."

"I can't begin to tell you how unnerving it is to have someone just appear in front of you. Just like that," Tara said as she snapped her fingers for emphasis, "from out of nowhere."

"That will stop when ya get a better grip on your gifts. I remember when I was your age and it happened to me," Maggie said with a chuckle. "Luckily I had me ma to explain it all. Don't ya have anyone?" When Tara shook her head, she sighed and shrugged her shoulders. "I'll tell ya what. Why don't I spend a little time with ya and show ya what I know? Would ya like that?"

"If I learn what you know, will the surprises stop? Will the fear end?" Tara asked with a voice that was full of hope.

Maggie wished she could be positive that learning would be all Tara needed, but until she better understood the girl's abilities and gifts, she really couldn't be certain.

"Most likely things will calm down for ya," Maggie said with less conviction than she liked. There was something about this girl that she couldn't put her finger on and hoped would come to light as time passed. Whatever it was, she suspected turmoil and danger accompanied it.

"I think I've met my savior," Tara said softly.

The relief in Tara's voice touched Maggie's heart. She reached over and lightly pinched Tara's cheek before moving to Sugar and gently caressing her neck.

Maggie smiled broadly, "The sun is down, the moon is out, and I feel like howling! Take me home, lass. We'll start your lessons the day after tomorrow."

****

Tara listened to the grandfather clock in the corner chime the hour. It was five a.m. and the sun was just peeking over the horizon. The tiled kitchen floor felt cool against her bare feet as she made her way to the coffee maker. Her senses heightened to the aroma of freshly brewed coffee while her movements were slow and deliberate as she filled her mug with the rich, dark liquid. Mornings were always special to her. It was a time when she could be alone with her thoughts uninterrupted while most of the world still slumbered. Getting up at this hour was a habit she acquired while living in Manhattan. Now it was no longer necessary to rise so early to catch the peace and tranquility of the day, but the habit was a solid one that she chose not to abandon.

Not long after she had finished pouring her second cup of coffee the telephone rang. Its shrill ring startled her and she knocked over a nearby floor plant while getting up.

"What a mess!" She shouted to on one in particular as she rushed to grab the receiver out of its cradle.

Hello?" Her frustration when she answered was distinct.

"What's the matter?" Dennis asked, immediately on the alert. He was accustomed to a bright and bubbly response on the mornings he telephoned.

"My clumsy butt tripped over a plant on my way to answer the phone," Tara said in a soothing tone.

At the youthful age of twenty-two Dennis managed to make junior partner in the graphics company he'd worked in since he participated in a school internship program at the age of sixteen. Between the pressures of his new position, and the self-imposed pressure of being head of the family while their father was away, his cup was full. She didn't want to create unnecessary anxiety.

"I worry about you being by yourself. I thought maybe we should get you a dog or something. One that's trained," he mused.

"What about dad's allergies?" Tara asked.

"It's called Claritin," Dennis said with amusement. "Besides, he's gone more than he's home. He'll manage."

"I suppose it would be nice to have a household pet. Sugar's great, but she can't come in at night and snuggle," Tara mused. "Yes, a dog would be fantastic. Maybe a cat... or... what about both? Would a dog and cat get along together in the same house?"

The more she talked about getting a dog and a cat. The more she liked the idea.

"From watch dog to animal farm," Dennis chuckled.

"Now you sound like Mitch," Tara said in a tone that belied her displeasure.

"Speaking of Mitch, he called the other day," Dennis said, choosing to ignore his sister's change in attitude.

You won't believe it. He fell in love with this chick he met at school." There was hesitancy in his voice when he added, "It sounds pretty serious."

"No kidding!" she said louder and with more enthusiasm than intended while she worked at covering the myriad of emotions that were raging within her. "He always did like the girls. What makes you think it's serious?"

"He's thinking of proposing," Dennis replied.

Flashes of memory of Mitch flew before her. She recalled his kisses, his hugs, and his silly habit of eating the crust of the sandwich first and creating a small circle to pop into his mouth. He made eating a simple sandwich a ritualistic experience. He used to laugh and say it stemmed back to his childhood days but he never went further with the explanation.

"Good for him," she said with false enthusiasm that she prayed he wouldn't recognize.

"You're pretty cool about it," Dennis said with relief.

"Mitch and I have been over for some time," Tara explained. "I have no reason to be anything else."

The pitch of Tara's voice sounded slightly higher than normal to her. Did Dennis believe her? Better yet, did she believe herself? Was she really over Mitch?

"I thought you two might get back together, but I guess I was wrong," Dennis admitted. "It's good you're over him. He's my friend but he's not all that." He took a deep breath and changed the subject, "So, what's on your agenda today? Are you planning anything fun and interesting?"

As much as he enjoyed visiting his sister's home, he often wondered how she kept herself from going crazy with the constant quiet and isolation. It was such a drastic change from the hustle and bustle of Manhattan. He'd be out of his mind by now.

Tara proceeded to go into great detail about her new friend, Maggie. Dennis listened intently. He was pleased to hear she found a friend out there in no man's land and he encouraged her to cultivate it. He didn't feel comfortable with her being so isolated and alone. A friend nearby was good, no matter what the age difference.

She was placing the receiver in the cradle when Maggie entered without waiting for an invitation. Oddly, Tara wasn't offended by her new friend's familiarity and accepted it as part of her eccentricity. She was just thankful she'd decided to slip into a light cotton dress before coming downstairs and wasn't caught wearing her robe and slippers.

"All ready for the big day?" Maggie asked enthusiastically.

"I'm excited and a little nervous. Just what am I going

to be learning?" Tara replied.

"The basics, love. Just the basics and then you're on your own," The old woman bellowed over her shoulder as she led Tara into the living room.

It occurred to Tara that Maggie knew her way around her house as well as she did. She made a mental note to ask if Maggie had visited her grandmother in the past.

The two positioned themselves in on opposite ends of the antique sofa that had only recently been delivered from the furniture restorer. Maggie reached into a bag she brought with her and pulled out a white candle, oil, matches, a bag of dried leaves, sticks of incense and an incense holder.

When everything was carefully arranged on the coffee table Maggie turned to Tara and said, "These are the basics for the first step to the gift. I want ya to pay close attention to what I'm saying and doing."

Tara nodded, unable to take her eyes off the spread before her.

"Now," Maggie continued, "we start with this white candle. Ya shouldn't meditate with anything but white in the beginning. The colors bring different energy. That's all ya need to know about it for now. We can do colors another time. Just remember. Use only white candles. Got that?"

Tara nodded again.

Maggie grabbed Tara's hands and gently pressed the candle in her palm while she dabbed a little oil in Tara's other palm and then guided her hands into action.

"Good," Maggie said with satisfaction. "Now, I want ya to take this candle and hold it carefully while ya rub some oil on it. That will make it burn longer. Ya start in the middle an' work your way to the ends. Like this, see?"

Maggie's large, calloused hands were remarkably gentle and dexterous as they directed her eager pupil.

When they finished with the candle, the old woman secured it in a holder and moved toward the bag of dried leaves.

"This is called sage, 'tis for balancing the energies," she explained. "The Indians like to lay claim on it but we been using it back in the old country since the beginning of time. Ya can grow it in the garden. Now stand before me nice and straight with your arms out to your sides."

Tara obediently followed Maggie's instructions as she watched the old woman pull a few sage leaves from the bag, light them and then blow out the flame. The leaves billowed smoke, while emitting a pungent aroma that resembled marijuana. Tara coughed as Maggie waived the sage around her body, did the same to herself, and then waved it around the room. She snuffed the remaining lit sage in an ashtray and then lit the incense.

The smooth aroma of the incense curled and intertwined with the pungent aroma of the sage, creating an exotic blend. The room felt still and warm. It was as if a blanket of security covered the entire space. The songs of birds flittered through the open window, accentuating the sense of peace pouring though her.

"Now we're ready," Maggie said as she straightened her back. "Sit back nice and straight. Rest your hands on your thighs, nice and peaceful. Now close your eyes and make your mind as still as ya can. Don't control the thoughts. Just let them flow in and out and stay that way until I say stop. Got it?"

Tara didn't respond. She was afraid that if she moved a muscle she would break the magic in the room. Time stood still while the aromatic essence in the room filled her nostrils. Her head felt heavier and heavier while her body experienced a floating sensation similar to when she had entered the clouds and met Liam. Liam... she hadn't thought of that experience in a while.

She was floating through the clouds. She felt light and free. Wisps of clouds prevented her from seeing below, but she was certain if she could she would find the earth a very small ball off in the distance.

As movement slowed down, the clouds slowly dispersed and she found herself standing in an enormous field of colorful flowers and tall grass that reached mid-calf. The aromatic blending of flowers of all varieties created a scent that was nothing short of wonderful while the grass tickled her legs. She breathed in freely while looking down at the hem of her dress. Its hem settled about an inch above the top of the grass, leaving her calf and bare feet exposed to be caressed and tickled by the softness of thick blades of emerald green.

Liam stood before her with his hand outstretched, beckoning her to approach. She did so willingly.

The sensation she experienced all around her was one of love and happiness. Everything was bright and cheerful. She neither saw nor felt a speck of darkness. Surprisingly, the absence of dark didn't bother her eyes like one might think. Her surroundings were bright but not exceeding her level of tolerance.

"Greetings. You are welcome and loved," said Liam as she moved next to him.

"Where am I?" she asked.

"You are in a space-time that parallels your own," he replied.

"It's so bright and happy," she mused.

"This is true," he said. "Where there is Light, darkness cannot abide."

"Is this where we go when we die?" she asked. "Where is everyone?"

"The location one goes to upon exiting their body vehicle is not always the same for each soul. This location is what you might consider an anteroom should it be in your home. From here one can move in a variety of directions," he explained.

She looked around her but saw only flowers and grass.

"Where is everyone?" she asked.

"Do you wish to see humans?" he asked patiently.

She nodded.

"Do you have a particular sight you wish to see or shall I select one for you?" he continued.

"Surprise me," she giggled.

"Very well," he said as he waived his hand in the air and their surroundings began to swirl.

They remained in a field but the flowers were fewer in number and far less vibrant. The velvety grass grew coarse against her tender flesh. The sky was hazy and the clouds were thick and laden with an impending storm. The sun's rays struggled to twist and weave around their massive bulk with minimal success.

To Tara's surprise and amazement, a woman who looked to be about twenty and a woman who was clearly approaching middle age appeared before her. Dressed in period clothing of the late eighteen hundreds, they were picking wildflowers without giving her a speck of notice. It was as if she wasn't even there, yet she could clearly feel the ground beneath her feet and the moistness in the air.

"They cannot see you," Liam explained, as if knowing her thoughts.

Taken aback by the fact that she'd said nothing, Tara could only nod. She wanted to know more about why they couldn't see her, but her thoughts and her tongue wouldn't coordinate. She was positive he was able to know her thoughts but since he didn't volunteer any more information, she focused on the scene before her.

As the younger of the two women stood up to stretch her back Tara gasped. She was looking at her identical twin! With the exception of the difference in clothing and hair style there was nothing to differentiate one from the other.

The woman looked directly at Tara with knit brows.

"What is it, lass?" asked the middle-aged woman.

"I feel eyes on me," replied the younger woman.

The middle-aged woman stood up and peered in Tara's direction.

"'Tis probably best to head back to me cottage. Those dang shadow people are sneaky. We have what we need," she said briskly.

The younger woman looked long and hard at Tara for a bit longer before heaving a sigh, picking up her basket, and following her companion across the field.

"Who are they?" Tara asked. "She looks just like me."

She turned to where Liam had been standing to await his reply only to find him no longer there. She had no idea where she was or how to leave. Panic filled her. Would she be stuck in this space-time plateau?

"Liam!" she called. "Liam, come back!"

Unsure what to do, she ran across the field in the direction the two women had gone. She had almost caught up with them when she stopped short. The view before her was so amazingly spectacular that she forgot all else while she admired acres and acres of garden. Along the far edge of it she could see an orchard hosting a variety of fruit trees. With science at his disposal, she was aware of no agriculture farmer able to produce a harvest as healthy and abundant as what lay before her. It was impressively breathtaking.

Tara stood watching as the women carefully picked their way through the carefully tended garden toward a quaint looking cottage on the farthest end. It was too far away for Tara to make out much more than its shape and color, but she inherently knew it was well kept and inviting.

A large black steed came racing up the long drive to the left of the cottage. The women waived their greeting and picked up speed to meet him. The three disappeared into the little cottage just before the scene faded away and Tara found herself once again in a field of brilliant flowers and tall emerald grass. She welcomed the softness of the blades against her skin once again.

Liam appeared before her and bowed slightly.

"What did I just see?" she asked earnestly.

"You have only to remember, dear one," he replied. "It

is all within you."

"Time's up," Maggie whispered so she wouldn't startle her.

"Already? It seems like we only just started," Tara exclaimed as she did her best to subdue the urge to complain about being dragged back to reality so abruptly.

Maggie chuckled, "That's normal but we were quiet for almost an hour."

"Really?" Tara asked with wonder. "That's so incredible."

Her words drawled with satisfaction as she stretched her body in a cat-like manner. Still feeling the effects of the meditation, Tara's body was slow to respond and move about.

The room felt chillier than when they began so Tara walked to the window to close it. She was shocked to see the position of the sun in the sky. It backed Maggie's claim of their meditation length.

"I saw something very odd in my meditation," Tara said.

"Truly?" Maggie asked. "Would ya like to tell me?"

"It was very strange, almost like a dream," Tara began. "First I was with my spirit guide, Liam. We were in this beautiful field of flowers. Their colors were incredibly vibrant and their scent was magnificent. I asked him about it and he said it was like what we would refer to as an anteroom. It led to many places."

"Aye, I know that place well," Maggie said with a nod of her head and a warm, knowing smile.

"Then he asked me if I wanted to see more," Tara continued. "Of course I did. That's when it got weird."

"How so?" Maggie asked.

"Well, he took me. At least I think he took me. However it happened, the field of flowers grew far less vibrant and sparser. The grass became brittle and sharp on my bare skin – similar to the feel of our fields here. Out of the blue two women appeared. They were dressed like they dressed in the late eighteen hundreds and were searching through the field and selecting flowers to put in their basket."

"That doesn't sound so odd," Maggie mused. "I do that meself on a regular basis."

"No, it wasn't that. It was the younger of the two women. She looked just like me! It was like I was looking into a mirror or something," Tara explained. "Do you think they were real, or did I make them up?"

Maggie thought for a moment and then said, "I'm not exactly sure, lass. There's something about what ya saw that feels mighty familiar. It's like I've seen it meself in a dream and then forgotten it."

"There's more. I followed them across the field to a quaint cottage that had an incredibly gigantic garden. It was the size of five football fields. What was even more impressive was the size and health of the plants growing in it," Tara said passionately. "It had to have been my imagination. No one produces vegetables like that these days."

"Ah, but they did at one time," Maggie said. "I wonder if ya went back in time a bit."

"But, I saw me there," Tara said.

"True, ya did," Maggie sighed, "that I cannot explain. It feels to me that what ya saw was real but I cannot make sense of why ya would put yourself in the mix. The mind is a powerful mysterious thing. Perhaps the reason or the message will come clear in time."

"Do you think it was a message?" Tara asked. Being unfamiliar with meditation she had no idea what to expect but she certainly hadn't expected a vision of this nature and the possibility of this vision being a message of some sort.

"'Tis not uncommon to receive messages that we cannot decipher right away when we go into meditation," Maggie explained.

Tara giggled, "The woman with my double spoke like you."

"Did she now?" Maggie smiled.

Maggie stayed for a late morning tea and shared some of the area gossip. Tara wasn't in a hurry for her to leave. She found the old woman unique and charming. When she finally did depart Tara wandered back into the parlor and stretched out on the sofa. She wasn't accustomed to napping but the excitement of entertaining and the relaxation of deep meditation left her in need of one. She drifted off into a deep sleep and remained there until it was almost dinner time.

FOUR

Tara could barely focus on her activities around the house while she watched for Maggie's return. She regretted not getting a phone number from her new friend. She didn't even know exactly where she lived. When Maggie asked her to drive her home she insisted they stop the car at the spot where they'd met. She insisted her house was just on the other side of the trees and she could use a 'good stretch of the legs'.

Tara watched Maggie disappear into the trees and followed her for as far as she felt comfortable going in unfamiliar surroundings but could see no signs of a house anywhere. She thought of going to town and questioning if anyone could direct her to Maggie's place, but since Maggie said she liked to keep to herself Tara doubted she'd approve.

They'd made no specific schedule or plans for their next meeting. She had no recourse but to wait for her new friend to return.

Working in the garden was one of the best ways to take Tara's mind off her impatient expectation of Maggie. She straightened her back and proudly surveyed her handiwork. Long straight rows of green peeked above the rich dark soil with robust health. Without warning the plants came alive with vibrant light circling the leaves and stalks while darting back and forth. It reminded her of a light show she saw in the city. It was beautiful. Then, as quickly as it started, it stopped. Unruffled, she reached for the garden hose and sprayed the plants with gentle care while Sugar frolicked playfully around the nearby paddock. Her mane and tail flowed freely as she leaped over the newly fallen tree in her paddock and turned to do it again. Tara decided not to remove the tree after it crashed to the ground like thunder during the last severe storm since her unusual horse clearly took delight in playing with it.

Sometimes Tara wondered what Sugar's personality would have been like had she remained in the stable with the other horses. She'd heard horses acted more aloof when in a herd. She'd certainly come out of her shell since the move. Dennis claimed the horse was confused about what she was. Tara thought he was probably right.

The mare approached the fence, snorting and stamping her powerful hoofs into the soft earth. Tara turned the hose off, set it down and walked carefully through the rows of vegetables to where Sugar struggled to reach the delicious looking fare on the other side.

"Oh no you don't girl, that's people food!" Tara chuckled as she reached the horse and gave her a big hug.

"What's people's food?" giggled a voice that sounded like it might be coming from a little girl or a very little person.

Tara's head whipped around while she searched for the owner of the voice.

"I'm over here," it said.

She followed the voice to the edge of her garden to the mounds of earth sporting pumpkin plants that were beginning to bloom. Seeing something scurry beneath a thick yellowish-orange pumpkin blossom, she bent down to investigate.

A gasp escaped her lips when she found herself looking at the tiniest little woman she'd ever imagined. A Barbie doll was bigger than this little snit of a thing.

"Size doesn't make the person, you know," spat the little woman.

"I'm sorry," Tara stuttered.

It figured that this creature could hear her thoughts.

"I'm a nature fairy," the little creature explained.

Doing her best to control the urge to run away and call a psychiatrist, Tara asked politely, "Do you have a name?"

"My name is Celia, what's yours?" the fairy asked.

"I'm Tara," she replied.

"It's nice to meet you, Tara," Celia said as she flew up into the air until she was level with Tara's face.

"I had no idea fairies were real," Tara mused, more to herself than to Celia. "I wonder how much of the fairy tales we're told as children is really based on fact."

"Much more than you realize," Celia replied. "We have what you call fairy tales here too. In fact, it wasn't until I was grown and received my assignment that I discovered that humans were real. They have you portrayed as evil giants in many of our bedtime stories."

"Oh," Tara gasped, "how horrible."

"You have to admit than much of the human race is horrible," Celia said firmly.

"Not all of us," Tara said defensively.

"That's true," Celia replied. "You're not horrible," she said sweetly. "I like you."

"Why, thank you," Tara said with a grateful smile. "Have you been here long?"

"Oh yes," the fairy said eagerly. "I was here long before your ancestors the owned place. It was much lovelier then, but you're bringing it back to life. That's why I like you."

"How old are you?" Tara asked thoughtfully.

"Hmm. I'm not exactly sure," the fairy replied. "Time in our realm is different than in yours."

"You don't live in this realm?" Tara quizzed.

"Of course not," Celia said with a giggle. "I only come here once in a while. Most of the time I work from my side of the divider."

"Why are you here now?" Tara asked politely.

"I saw you in the field with that spirit and I wanted to meet you," Celia said.

"That was your field?" Tara asked with surprise.

"No. I don't own it. No one owns things like you humans tend to believe. It's part of my realm though," Celia explained with a hint of exasperation.

"Oh," Tara said with bewilderment.

"Oops, time to go," Celia said before popping out of sight before Tara's very eyes with no warning whatsoever.

Tara stood motionless for a long time while she debated about what just occurred. Had she been spending so much time away from the world that she'd finally lost her mind? First she has that incredible vision of herself back in the eighteen-hundreds and now this.

Maggie's reaction to her vision was so perplexed that she regretted telling her. Explaining the encounter with a fairy might just push the woman away completely. She decided to hold her tongue and just hope whatever was going on with her subsided now that she'd made a friend and would have companionship.

A flash caught the corner of her eye and she swirled quickly to see what it was. All was quiet with no sign of anyone or anything. She stood up, took a deep breath, and wiped her eyes. Enough was enough. She could either crumple in fear or get moving and find out what it was that was zipping around her place. It didn't matter whether it was good or bad. She had to find out what it was. If it was something bad she would deal with it when the time came.

The door on the ancient tool shed slowly creaked. Her arms and legs trembled as she carefully approached the weathered structure. She felt her heart pounding in the cavity of her head and her breathing thundered in her ears. She tried holding her breath to silence herself but it was all the louder when she resumed breathing. What if the intruder was waiting for her in there? Should she investigate or call the police? She armed herself with a rake that leaned against the building.

Leaning against the side of the building with the rake tight in her grip, she struggled to regain control of her body. Beads of sweat coated her forehead and her nerves threatened to flee her body at any moment. She wasn't sure her legs could support her one more minute.

The door creaked again.

With all the fortitude she could muster, Tara made her way toward the door. She was just about to enter when an enormous mountain cat swept past her. Its piercing yowl blended with Tara's shrill screeching at the startling confrontation. Her screams continued long after the beast disappeared into the tall grass of the fields. When her legs finally gave out, she crumbled to the ground.

"That's the biggest cat I've ever seen," she mumbled, not caring about the fact that there was no one to hear her. "That had to be the biggest cat I've ever seen! What was it doing here? What kind of cat was it? Could it have been a bobcat or mountain lion?"

When her legs finally felt strong enough to hold her again, she pulled herself up with the help of the rake handle. Standing quietly while she steadied herself, Tara heard a faint cry that resembled a peep. She stood perfectly still and strained her ears for the sound. When the cry came again it was muffled but distinct.

She walked cautiously into the shed and stopped with a start. Vomit gushed into her esophagus like lava from a volcano. She rushed outside in time to projectile vomit the entire contents of her stomach. When she finished, she leaned against the building and wiped at her face and nose as best she could with her hands.

Again she heard the small cry.

She steadied herself and started back inside, this time ready for the horror that waited.

Tara swung the door wide open to allow as much light as possible. She may have dreaded facing the torment inside but she dreaded even more the possibility of stepping on it due to insufficient lighting. Her feet tread carefully to avoid the fur and entrails scattered around the floor amidst large pools of blood. It looked like a massacre took place. She was surprised such a thing occurred without her hearing something from the onset. This was a fresh kill. She must have had one of her 'zone-out' moments without realizing it. The concern over lost time quickly left her as she covered her mouth and the little vomit she had left oozed between her fingers. The head of what was once a beautiful house cat lay inches from her feet. Its eyes stared blankly and its tongue protruded out of the corner of its mouth. Blood drenched its once fluffy gray fur. Six inches to its left was one of its front legs. Shocked and horrified, she couldn't endure the scene any longer. She rushed out of the shed and fell to her knees. Her body had a will of its own and even though she'd already emptied her stomach, it heaved and wretched anyway.

The action brought a semblance of relief. When she was able, she sat with her back braced against the building, struggling over what to do. The crying sounded fainter. She knew she had to reach whatever it was in there to help. That meant braving the horrible scene of blood and guts. She closed her eyes and prayed for strength. Her head grew light and a feeling of euphoria consumed her.

'Go in. You will be strong.'

Whether the voice in her head belonged to Liam and he was really speaking to her or she was imagining it on her own, it made her feel empowered and ready. Leaping to her feet, she entered the shed with deliberation. She moved steadily to the dusty old side cupboard without looking in the direction of the cat's remains. Pulling open a drawer, she yanked out a trash bag. She'd left her gloves in the garden so she searched for another pair and put them on. The cries were more distinct. She was able to pick up their location without even searching.

Grabbing a small transplanting spade, Tara walked to the cat's remains. She was the only one to do the job and the job had to be done. So be it. She took a deep breath to steady her nerves and her stomach and scooped all signs of the tragedy into the bag.

When she completed the horrendous task, she tied up the bag and set it outside the door before heading in the direction of the peeping cries. Pulling at some half full bags of garden fertilizer, she found a small bed of rags. Tucked within their folds were three tiny kittens that were barely able to walk. They were so young she was certain they had not yet been weaned. Without their mother they wouldn't last long.

Tara pulled a small basket from a hook on the wall and shook out the dust. She scooped up the kittens, rags and all, and placed them gently in the basket. On her way out of the shed, she stopped for a moment and stared at the bag containing the remains of the mother. How cruel life is at times. How mysterious and cruel. What will these poor baby kittens do without a mother? What was she supposed to do with them? She knew nothing about how to care for them, absolutely nothing.

She longed for Maggie.

The tiny creatures squirmed in the basket, snuggling each other for comfort and assurance. Tara noticed one was lethargic. It was barely moving or breathing. She rushed into the house with her basket and set it on the kitchen table. Scurrying into the laundry room, she returned with a bundle of fresh rags for the basket. She gently took each kitten out and placed it on the table. They were more mobile than she'd anticipated and made their way toward the table's edge, each in a different direction while their crying grew more pronounced.

Tara quickly dumped the basket upside down to remove the old rags. The jerking action loosened more dirt and dust and it settled on her table. She decided this was a poor choice of location to do this, but it was too late to stop now. She barely caught each escapee before it reached the edge of the table. The scent of their mother left the basket along with the old rags and they cried out for her with loud wails.

"It sure looks like you have your hands full, where did you get these little guys?" Dennis said as he came up behind her and slid his arm affectionately around her slender waist. Tara was so busy struggling to take care of the kittens she never even heard her brother arrive. She laid her head back against his chest, relieved to have reinforcement for the situation.

"It's been a nightmare," she moaned. "There was this enormous cat that was bigger than anything I've seen before. It killed the mother in the tool shed. What a mess." Tara shuddered for emphasis. "I've no idea what to do with such tiny creatures but I couldn't just leave them there. How will they survive? They need nursing, that's for sure. How am I supposed to pull that off?"

"Do you have any droppers in the house?" her brother asked in a steady tone that helped to soothe his sister's mania. "You know, like an eye dropper?"

"There's one in the valerian jar. It's almost empty." Tara replied. She was happy to have someone take charge.

"Go get it and clean it out thoroughly. I'll warm up a little milk and we'll see if we can get these little guys to quiet down," Dennis said.

He released his hold on Tara and the two went about their designated duties. Before long, the tiny kittens where satisfied and quiet. Tara smiled contentedly at the basket of sleeping beauties.

"So, now sis, what say we get ourselves a cold drink and go out on the patio while you tell me all about what's happened since last we spoke," Dennis suggested. "Start from the beginning and don't leave a thing out. This should be interesting."

The two poured themselves some newly made iced tea and headed for the patio so Tara could tell her story.

****

It was two weeks before Maggie came around again. Tara abandoned her watch after the first week and dove back into her day to day duties with gusto. The kittens proved to be a handful. Her days stayed full of their care, Sugar's care, the duties of the household and its needed repairs. Sleep felt like a luxury.

When Maggie did finally arrive it was just in time for

dinner. She boisterously laughed and teased and carried on with Tara as if the two were longtime friends and she had only visited the day before.

Maggie showed little surprise when she saw the kittens. It was as if she knew of their existence all along. She held each one in her hands and did what she called 'scanning of their bodies'. Maggie could actually picture in her mind the inside of a person or an animal. Although she was never educated in the medical field, she was able to pick up on abnormalities in a body and instinctively know whether the affliction required a doctor's care or a simple home remedy.

"This kitten's got a weak heart. I'm surprised he lived. You've got the touch," Maggie stated with assurance as she stroked the tiny kitten and chuckled at the purr that sounded far too loud for such a tiny thing.

"I'm surprised he lived too. His breathing got so shallow. He had me worried. If Dennis had not shown up when he did I don't think any of them would have lived. I was at a complete loss at what to do," Tara's said with a voice filled with emotion.

"Oh, I don't know about that. Ya seem to have the knack for it. I think ya would've figured it out mighty quick if ya had to. Have more faith in yourself," Maggie said.

There was a gentleness in Maggie's voice and eyes that somehow didn't match her energetic frame. Tara looked from the tiny kitten with the loud boisterous purr and then to the feisty old woman with her soft gentle voice and smiled.

Maggie placed the kitten on the floor, stood up and stretched. As she made her way to the living room, she called back, "Let's get to work".

Tara followed obediently. She hadn't noticed the large cloth sack Maggie carried until the old woman reached inside and pulled out a thick, leather bound book. Tara stretched forward to take a closer look. The book showed years of wear. The binding was worn thin and the pages were yellowed. At the end of a long black ribbon that was glued within the binding of the book was an octagon shaped crystal that measured one and one-half inches in length and one inch in diameter.

Thinking the crystal looked out of place, she couldn't resist asking Maggie about it. Maggie simply shrugged her shoulders and said it had been part of the book since before her birth and the birth of her mother. She assumed it was what helped keep the magic within the pages. Tara marveled over how much loving care Maggie displayed as she dexterously turned the pages until she found the section she sought.

"This book's been in me family for generations," she said reverently. "It tells the secrets of the ages. It tells the secrets of the gift. I want ya to have it, lass. I've no family to give it to and the secrets can't be lost. Besides, we share the same last name. I'll bet we're related somehow."

"Shirt-tail cousins," Tara said with amusement.

"Perhaps," Maggie replied.

Maggie gently laid the open book on the table before Tara. The large print almost jumped off the pages. The Gothic style lettering was clean and crisp. Tara slid her hand lightly over the pages and felt a warm vibration in her palms. Maggie gave a full bellied laugh when Tara jerked away with a startled look.

The women made themselves comfortable on the sofa while Maggie explained the book's history. She told of her ancestors and their connection to the world of magic and spirits. The family was revered at times and persecuted at others, but through the ages the gift, the wisdom, and the book was passed down from generation to generation.

The two spent the rest of the day pouring through the book. It amazed Tara how sensible, simple, and clear the information was. It covered topics from healing with herbs, to casting a spell, to conjuring the spirit world. Tara thought she'd burst with excitement. She couldn't wait to sit down and read through its entirety. She asked Maggie if she'd read it all and the old woman nodded. It was a staple in her family.

Maggie grew serious, "Ya must promise to take care

of this book. 'Tis older than this old house. Don't let anyone touch it, not even your brother. Promise?

Tara nodded in agreement. There was something sacred about the whole scene. She felt like she was pledging before God. She would keep the secrets of the book close to her until told otherwise.

When Maggie got up to leave, Tara ran into the coat room to get her car keys to drive her home. When she had returned to the living room, it was quiet. The breeze gently tugged at the draperies through the open windows and the dusk outside them showed a bright orange skyline lining the tree tops. There was no sign of her friend. She'd left as quickly and quietly as she'd arrived.

Pausing only briefly to ponder on the mysteries of Maggie, she settled herself back onto the sofa to further investigate the treasured book before her.

She found connotations for invoking both good and evil spirits, as well as one to raise the dead. This surprised her. Why would Maggie's ancestors want to conjure an evil spirit or raise the dead?

Fascinated by the pull of the words on the page, she softly whispered the Bring Forth the Dead Incantation. A cold chill swept over her and her temples throbbed. She carefully placed the ribbon down the interior binding of the pages and closed the book shut. The crystal didn't look quite so out of place as it lay against the bottom of the pages. In fact, there was so much room between the size of the cover and the size of the pages that crystal tucked right up into the gap when she set the book on end. It was a perfect fit.

Tara scoped the room for a place to put it. Maggie insisted she keep the book safe. The second-floor den had an enormous bookcase built into the wall. If she placed it on the top shelf it could easily blend in with the array of books of all shapes and sizes that were stuffed, shoved and crammed in rows from floor to ceiling. She felt a little light headed when she stood up. She couldn't decide if it was from the power emanating from the book she held close to her chest or simply because she stood up too fast. Whatever the reason, she took the time to stand still and wait for her equilibrium to come back before heading off to the den.

****

With the book safely hidden in plain sight, Tara's body felt the hours of the day. Her muscles ached and her eyelids were heavy. She made her way back toward the kitchen for a cup of hot herbal tea which she intended to enjoy while snuggling in bed. Half way down stairs she changed her mind about the tea. She was too tired to make it. She was asleep in a matter of minutes after crawling beneath the covers.

Waves of light flew past as she floated beyond the clouds. The wings of angels surrounded her. Their light caressed her cheeks like a gentle kiss. Peace and tranquility flowed through and around her. She felt safe. Her body rocked and swayed as she continued to float with no particular destination in mind.

The clouds parted and she stood next to Liam. She smiled. Finding him here amongst the clouds and the angels somehow brought completion to the whole experience. She felt the bond between them. A familiar yet indescribable bond that was unlike anything she had with anyone else. His gentle eyes gazed into hers. She marveled how it was as if there was a space within them that was a world in itself. Liam looked down and she followed his gaze. Below her in a dimly lit cave lay a woman that looked exactly like her. She looked at Liam questioningly. He smiled and nodded before darkness returned.

****

She sat up in bed and reflected on her dream. She felt a strong need to write down what she could remember. She got out of bed, went into the den and sat at her computer. The words rushed forth so quickly her fingers could barely keep up. When she finished, she returned back to her bed and immediately fell into a deep, comfortable sleep.

****

A loud crash startled her out of the warmth of her slumber. Taking a moment to gather her wits about her, Tara looked for the source of the commotion. The morning sun announced the beginning of another beautiful day as it peeked merrily through the gaps in the drapes. Its haze of dusty particles hovered along beams of sunlight that tickled the faded roses on the wool carpet covering the majority of the bedroom floor. The room felt still as her eyes slowly focused.

She gasped at the loud crash again.

Leaping from the bed, she shoved her slender feet into her slippers, pulled on her robe with a quick rapid ease that required little thought, and tiptoed quietly toward the door. She grabbed the baseball bat propped in the corner of the room and hesitated only briefly before poking her head into the hall to look for intruders.

The long broad hallway sported memories of a time of grace, beauty and elegance. The faded wallpaper echoed laughter of children running from room to room playing hide and seek. She could almost hear the clicking of the housekeeper's heels as she made her rounds, or the soft rustling of party gowns as the women gracefully descended the elegant staircase toward the admiring eyes waiting below.

At one time, Tara's house was the main home of a grand estate in the pre-Civil war era. Her great, great grandfather originally emigrated to the south from Ireland after meeting and marrying a southern bell traveling abroad with her father. Having been raised in Connemara, he found southern weather intolerable. When he moved his wife and family north, he ordered a replica of his grand southern mansion built in the middle of the hilly farmland he'd purchased in hopes it would appease his wife and make up for some of the inconveniences found in the north verses the south.

It was the talk of the north. Tara knew little else about the estate but intended to do some research when time allowed.

When the crash sounded again she was able to tell it was coming from the den. She hurried cautiously down the hall and stopped short at the doorway. Her mouth fell open, but not a sound passed her trembling lips as she slowly took in the scene before her. The room was in total disarray. The curtains were shredded. The stuffing was out of the sofa and scattered about. The once graceful antique etched glass doors of the wall length bookcase lay shattered on the floor with pieces of the antique glass projected as far as the other side of the large room. It was as if an explosion occurred. Papers were scattered about and long deep claw marks ran along the surface of the desktop. Her laptop was opened and upside down on the floor.

The book Maggie entrusted her with was the only thing in the room that was exactly as she left it. She pulled it off the shelf and hugged it to her chest while lowering herself carefully onto the remnants of the sofa. She sat staring in disbelief, unable to grasp what occurred or even how it happened.

One of her kittens braved the destruction and pounced up next to her. She stroked the feline gently as she caught a brief glimpse of a dark figure flash by. The room was suddenly cold enough for her to see her breath. An icy chill crept slowly and deliberately up her spine. She sat completely still, held her breath, and listened to her heart pounding against her ear drums. A small black ball materialized and hovered close to her face. Slowly, deliberately, it grew bigger and bigger. As it grew she was able to see inside it. The creature looking out was like nothing she had ever seen before. It reeked of evil.

Paralyzed, she emitted a shrill scream.

Unable to move or take her eyes off the creature, Tara

could only watch out of the corner of her eyes as a bright white beam of light formed in the corner of the room. Out of its brightness walked Liam. Calmly, deliberately, he moved until he stood between her and the growing black ball with its gruesome creature.

He remained calm as he turned to her and quietly asked, "Do you desire my assistance?"

Tara feebly nodded her head, still too stunned to do much else. Liam turned quickly, no longer serene in his actions. He raised his arms high above his head and spread his palms wide open before swirling them to form symbols in the air. Bright light bounced everywhere as Liam spoke in a powerful, clear and authoritative manner, "By the power of the Great One, I command you be gone!" He repeated this command three times, each time with more strength and force that repeatedly punched the black ball. Within moments the ball shrank into nothingness.

Liam turned back around and addressed her calmly, "It appears you have unlocked the doors to darkness. We ask that you be more patient and cautious in your journey down the path of knowledge. All things come in time."

Without warning, he raised his arms high above his head. This time he formed a small glowing ball of firelight. It hovered overhead in the center of the room, spinning rapidly while heat permeated the room, warming her throughout her body and immediately calming her and bringing her back to her senses.

Liam's smile shone brightly as he bowed slightly. He retrieved the small glowing ball and tucked it into the folds of his robe before walking regally back into the ball of light he'd arrived in. She watched in awe as the glowing light that contained Liam faded into nothingness, leaving her still hugging Maggie's book in silent stillness until the sound of the purring cat next to her broke through. She rose slowly and walked to the door, stopping to take another look of the shredded room before returning to her bed.

****

As the old claw foot bathtub filled with hot, bubbly water Tara examined her face in the mirror. Her eyes looked hollowed and sunken. Her cheekbones protruded a little too much and her usually thick and lustrous lips looked pale and thin. The coloring of her face had a yellowish hue. She was reminded of the corpses laid out in funeral homes. She turned on the water in the old pedestal sink and splashed cool water over her cheeks in an attempt to add some color. Patting it dry with a soft towel she examined herself again. This time, her eyes where bright, her ruby lips thick and rich and her skin a glowing pink. Her full cheeks radiated the ruddy health that she was known to display. She shook her head. These halluci- nations were unnerving.

She stood motionless for a moment while she went over the medications she was still taking, a sleeping pill once in a while and some Ibuprofen. Surely these wouldn't be caus- ing such hallucinations. She decided she'd better make an ap- pointment with the doctor as soon as possible. Something was wrong. Removing her pajamas, she lowered herself be- neath the steaming bubbles and soaked for the better part of an hour.

The long soothing bath did wonders for calming her trembling nerves and restoring her spirits. Bouncing in her usual perky manner into the kitchen, she swung open the re- frigerator door and groaned. Horror of horrors, there was no creamer for her coffee. She slammed the door shut and leaned against it with her arms folded over her chest. Life changed so drastically since she inherited her house. Most of it was wonderful but there were aspects that bothered her, such as the inconvenience of not being able to run to the corner store or have something delivered. She just couldn't tolerate cof- fee without creamer. Her unsuccessful search for a non-dairy substitute in the cupboard forced her to start her day with tea and a wedge of lemon. She would have passed altogether but on this particular morning some sort of caffeine jolt was in order.

After sipping her tea and munching on an English muffin, she decided to make a trip to the local store for a few supplies before tackling the clean-up job that awaited her in the den upstairs. She did her major shopping on a monthly basis in the nearby city but frequented the local country store or went into the small town for the basics such as milk, bread and creamer.

She saddled her mare. The prospect of bonding with nature for a while was exciting. She found riding at a casual pace fantastic therapy for stress and tenseness.

As she gazed out over the hillside, the beauty of the day flowed before her with grace and ease. The countryside was filled with a kaleidoscope of colors. Sinking deeper into the saddle, she melded her body to Sugar's graceful gate and relaxed in anticipation of a peaceful journey to the local store.

As they reached a small grove of trees, Tara chuckled in amusement at a small family of squirrels as they scurried about collecting their nuts and taking them back to their nest. They were absorbed in their tasks and oblivious to her presence. The squirrels scattered when Sugar picked up her gate, bringing Tara's attention back to the path ahead. She often gave the mare her head on their rides, allowing her to go at the pace that suited her mood at the time. She could feel Sugar's body preparing for action and adjusted herself in preparation for wild abandonment on the stretch before them. This was her mare's favorite spot. The ground was flat and solid with minimal debris. It allowed Sugar the opportunity to put her powerful limbs into action without worry of injury. Tara's hair fell from the loosely tied knot on her head and flew freely down her back as they raced like the wind.

Out of the next grove of trees sprung an enormous wolf. The startled mare reared on her hind legs while Tara struggled to maintain her seating. The wolf looked just as startled as it stood motionless, staring. Sugar continued to rear and stomp, prancing away while Tara fought for control. The beast continued to stand motionless and stare. Sugar finally calmed down enough to satisfy Tara but stayed coiled to race away at a moment's notice.

This was her first encounter with a wolf and Tara wasn't sure if she should run or stand and face the creature. If she ran, would the wolf consider them prey and hunt them down? If they stood firm would it become confused and leave them alone? She just didn't know. While she was debating what to do the wolf disappeared into the grove.

Before Tara could regain her composure, a tall slender man appeared on the path. His sleek, fastidious attire emitted an air of prosperity. He led an enormous black steed that dwarfed her mare in comparison. The steed's long, silken black mane flowed casually as the gelding tossed his head and flicked his tail. His broad nostrils fluttered as he moved closer to Sugar.

The proud swagger in the stranger's walk, combined with the lock of jet black hair that fell teasingly over his brow, gave him a youthful appearance. It was the steel grey eyes that bore into her that spoke of wisdom and knowledge beyond his years. A chill ran up Tara's spine and the hairs stood on her neck as she shifted uncomfortably in the saddle. She felt as if he looked into her soul. She cleared her throat uncomfortably as a smile spread across his chiseled face. His straight, sturdy looking teeth glimmered in the afternoon sun. Her heart skipped a beat and her stomach fluttered. She had never responded in such a way to anyone before and wasn't sure what to make of it.

"Good afternoon, my name is Brandon. Brandon Wagner," he said with a distinct southern drawl. He extended his hand toward her with a casual grace but Sugar's prancing prevented Tara from reciprocating. Brandon raised his eyebrows and stepped back, "It appears I've startled your mare, my apologies."

"Sugar stop!" Tara barked.

She sounded a little more agitated than she intended. Her nerves were frazzled. She quickly assessed this tall, lean yet well-formed man. He was good looking but not extraordinarily so. Why did she react in this way? Maybe it was the way his eyes bore into her. She felt exposed in some way. Yet, oddly enough, it also gave her a feeling of anticipated excitement.

"We just encountered an enormous wolf," she said nervously. "Did you see it?"

"I didn't realize there were wolves in these parts," he replied thoughtfully. "Enormous you say?"

Tara's agitation grew steadily as Brandon's piercing eyes continued to watch her struggle to regain control of the high-spirited mare. Sugar never behaved like this and was at a loss at what to do next. Without knowing how he managed, she watched Brandon's strong hands at Sugar's head holding her fast to quiet her. His slender, well-manicured fingers gently stroked her mare's neck and Tara watched as she visibly relaxed. She stared at Brandon's hands for a long time. When she finally looked up, she was again taken aback by the intensity of those steel gray orbs. She quickly averted her attention to the black beast pawing at the earth behind him.

"Your horse is anxious to get moving and I need to be on my way. It was nice meeting you," she said.

Brandon's black hair tossed freely and his white teeth sparkled he as gave her a broad smile and said, "I didn't catch your name."

"I didn't give it," Tara snapped, surprising herself with the crisp reply.

"No you didn't," Brandon said as he bowed deeply while still wearing the smile.

Tara was suddenly ashamed of her lack of manners.

"I'm sorry," she stammered, "I don't know what got into me. My name is Tara and this is my mare, Sugar."

"It's a pleasure to meet you Tara," Brandon nodded his head toward the mare, amused to be introduced to the horse as well as the human, "and you too Sugar. May I ask what brings you out into this remote part of the country?"

"We're on our way to the country store. This is the quickest route," she explained.

"You live nearby?" he asked.

"On the O'Shea estate," she replied and then instantly scolded herself for divulging this information to a stranger.

"Ah, the O'Shea estate," he said thoughtfully. "If my information serves me correctly, that place was vacant for some time and in need of a considerable amount of repair."

"You're partially correct. It was only vacant for a few months before my father and I moved in," she volunteered. "As for repairs, it's definitely in need of them. My grandmother didn't keep up with it like she should have, but with some TLC and elbow grease it's turning out to be gorgeous."

"So you're an O'Shea," he said while studying her closer.

"Did you know my grandmother?" she asked.

"I know of the estate. It's a bit secluded," he said as his eyes bore into her. "That doesn't bother you?"

Tara squirmed uncomfortably. For a brief moment she'd relaxed and allowed herself to enjoy light conversation with this stranger, but his comment about her being secluded reminded her of her potential vulnerability. She studied him long and hard, trying to read any hidden meaning behind the words. His eyes never flinched and his smile never wavered. Either he made his comment in innocent interest or he possessed the best poker face she ever encountered.

"I have my father and brother, plus we get visitors so I don't feel at all secluded. In fact, I value and appreciate any quiet time I might have!" She lied.

Her father was on the other side of the world and other than an occasional visit from Maggie, there was no company for some time. Dennis hadn't even been by in two weeks, but she didn't feel comfortable letting this stranger know the truth. Besides, Dennis planned on taking time from work and said he would spend it helping her with some repair work on the house. She expected him at the end of the week.

"I'll have to excuse myself now, err... Brandon," she stammered. "I really need to get back or I'll be missed."

Another lie.

"No problem," Brandon's twinkling smile didn't match the intensity of his steel grey eyes as he bowed and stepped aside. "It was a pleasure to meet you."

Tara tipped her head in a short nod and smile awkwardly in his direction as she spurred her mare into action. She couldn't get away quick enough. She wished she knew how to reach Maggie. So many frightening things were happening. She thought about her destroyed den and the horrible creature in the ball and finally the enormous wolf. She needed to see Maggie. Maggie would know what to do, she was certain of it.

As she approached the main road leading to the small country store she spotted her new friend. With arms laden with groceries, Maggie was making her way to a small pull cart. Tara spurred Sugar forward and was at her side in no time. She slid from the saddle and immediately set out helping Maggie transfer the bundle of bags from her arms into the small pull cart.

"Ya came just in time," Maggie sighed with gratitude. "Old Mr. Roberts loaded me up, but for the life of me it was a mystery how to undo it all." She stretched her back with relief as the last bag was placed in the cart. "Good lord lass, ya look as if you've seen a ghost. What's the matter?" Tara opened her mouth to speak but before she could utter a word, Maggie continued. "Oh no, ya didn't! Gods save us. Ya read the incantation for the dead, didn't ya?"

Maggie's acute insight took Tara aback.

"I... I'm not sure," she stammered guiltily. "I think I might have. I read a lot last night. I read something that made me feel icy cold, so I stopped."

Maggie moaned in despair, "Did ya forget lass? Did ya forget to pay attention to the markings on the pages? The markings tell ya where ya can't read! Did ya read the marked pages?"

Frustration mixed with fear and the implications of what she did hit Tara.

"I don't know," she whined. "I don't know, Maggie. I just read. It was all so fascinating. I didn't look for markings.   I... I forgot about them."

Her heart twisted in a knot when it struck her that her fascination with Maggie's book may have been the cause for the nightmare Liam saved her from.

Maggie looked at Tara long and hard before patting her cheek reassuringly.

"What's done is done," she said with a sigh of resignation. "Let's walk together while ya tell me what's been going on. It just so happens I planned on paying ya a visit after I picked up a few goodies for us to enjoy. I was actually heading to your place after I took my groceries home." Maggie gave Tara a broad, reassuring smile, "We can start our visit right now."

Tara immediately dove into telling Maggie the chain of events since she closed the book the night before. Maggie listened in silence. After hearing Tara's tale, she decided it might be best for her to stay a few nights at Tara's house.

Tara eagerly agreed.

****

The setting sun glowed bright orange as Tara's Mustang crawled along the dirt road leading to Maggie's little cottage. The narrow, barely discernible drive felt never-ending as it wound its way up the wooded hillside. When they finally reached a clearing, Tara caught her breath. Never had she seen such a beautiful setting. A small white European style cottage was nestled intimately amongst ancient oak and apple trees that were surrounded by fields of grass and wildflowers swaying in the light summer breeze like the ripples of the ocean.

"It's like a whole different world," Tara mused with fascination as she maneuvered her car down the seldom used drive.

"This old cottage has been in me family for generations just like your old house," Maggie smiled.

Tara looked at Maggie with surprise, "But your accent... I thought you were an immigrant."

Maggie chuckled and said softly, "I was born and raised in Ireland but me ancestors also settled here. Like you, I inherited the place a few years back." She smiled, "Come meet me family."

"I thought you had no one," Tara's tone showed her confusion.

Maggie laughed jovially, "I have a lovely family but not the kind of family ya would expect."

As the car rolled to a stop before the white stucco cottage with its rounded oak door, a large collie bounded off the inviting oversized porch to greet them. Maggie hopped out with surprising agility and rigorously fluffed its fur. To Tara's amazement, the lawn filled with animals of all kinds. Cats jumped down from the roof where they were sunning themselves, while so many birds swooped down from overhead it reminded Tara of the movie 'The Birds'. Butterflies landed on the hood of her car, a rabbit hopped onto the porch sniffing the air and a raccoon balanced himself along the drain pipes.

Maggie's eyes twinkled, "Come in and sit while I gather a few things."

Tara followed Maggie into the house and settled into an overstuffed chair near the unlit fireplace. She smiled warmly when the collie laid its head in her lap. Its soft moist nose pushed at her, demanding attention.

Maggie paid little notice to the creatures both in and out of her house as she busily gathered herbs and powders and put them in a pouch. The scent of drying herbs mingled with the wild flowers, while shadows danced merrily in the remnants of the sun that filtered through the leaves of the trees and the large airy windows into the great room.

"What do you plan on doing with all those herbs and spices?" Tara asked. She found it hard to contain her curiosity.

"I don't know what I'll need at your place, so 'tis best to be prepared," Maggie replied as she fastened the clasped on the sack she packed her herbs and spices into. "Now, let me get some change of clothes and personal essentials and we'll be leaving."

After disappearing into her bedroom and returning with a small overnight bag she stood and stared at the collie with a concerned expression on her face, "I've not left him for more than half a day."

Tara didn't hesitate. "Can't he come too? He's so sweet," she said as she scratched the top of his head.

"Do ya hear that Angus? She says you're sweet!" Maggie laughed with relief while Angus placed his paws on Tara's lap and pulled himself up to cover her face with kisses. "Come on, old boy, 'tis time to get going." Maggie closed up the windows and set two large buckets of some type of animal food out on the porch. "This should hold the critters over until I get back," she explained as they headed for the car.

Convincing Angus to enter the car took considerable effort but eventually everyone was settled and Tara was guiding the car back down the long drive.

"'Tis an adventure for old Angus," Maggie said as she scratched her canine companion's head. "'Tis the first he's been in a car since I moved here. He's got a low tolerance for things that move."

Maggie's house was at the end of a private road that was so seldom used it was debatable whether it could even be called a road in today's terms. Tara thought it more like a path winding up the hillside. Although she was unable to travel at any significant speed, she still had to swerve the car onto the shoulder when Angus tried to climb into the front with them. She had just regained steering when she was forced to slam on the brakes to avoid hitting an enormous wolf standing steadfast in the middle of the road. Its large yellow eyes reminded her of her previous encounter that day. Was it the same wolf?

Angus growled and snarled while fighting Maggie's powerful gripped as she struggled to control him. The wolf showed no fear as it walked up to Tara's opened window. She was grateful they had raised the top of the convertible as she rushed to close it just before his moist nose reached the glass. It was canvas, of course, but it gave them some semblance of a barrier between the beast and them.

The wolf pressed his mouth against Tara's window and displayed his broad, pointed teeth. Saliva trickled down the glass. When he finally backed away he threw his head high and howled. Tara's heart beat against her eardrums, drowning out most of Angus' snarling and growling that mixed with the demon wolf's piercing howl. She shuddered as chills ran through her body and her legs went weak. She was barely able to respond to Maggie's urging to drive off.

"Angus! Ya hush now!" Maggie commanded. "Come on, lass. Let's move out of here. Hurry up now!"

Tara was too traumatized with the situation to notice a faint clip of panic in Maggie's voice.

"I didn't think wolves approached people like that. Do you think he's rabid?" Tara asked. Her voice and hands trembled as she pressed hard on the gas.

"Let's just get going and worry about it later!" Maggie barked.

This time the old woman's agitation didn't go unnoticed.

The howling stopped and the wolf disappeared into the trees while Tara sped away as best she could with her low riding car on the makeshift road. As they rounded a corner she swerved the car again. This time was to avoid hitting Brandon and his horse. He was unruffled by the narrow escape and gave a bowing gesture as her car continued past him. Tara watched Brandon and his noble steed through her rear-view mirror until they were no longer in sight.

"Darn fool. That's how accidents happen! What's he doing way out here anyway?" Maggie shifted uncomfortably in her seat and pulled Angus closer to her, still not willing to release her grip. She remained quiet and deep in thought for the rest of the drive. Tara was grateful for the silence. She needed time to digest the day's events. It was all too frightening and unreal.

The sun dropped behind the hillside as they turned onto her driveway. Sugar raced to greet them and got quite a response from Angus. They stopped the car and let him out to run and familiarize himself with the grounds and the mare. The two animals danced and raced together in instant friendship. For a moment, Tara forgot about the day's events while she delighted in the scene.

Maggie stayed reserved but still smiled.

Tara parked the car in the circular driveway near the front door and immediately started pulling Maggie's belongings from the trunk. Her nostrils took in the rich aroma of herbs and spices the bag emitted as she lifted it. Maggie grabbed what Tara left behind and closed the trunk. She didn't immediately follow the young woman up the steps, taking a moment to assess the feel of the place. She sensed a slight shift in energy since her last visit. It left her feeling unsettled, yet she couldn't put her finger on exactly why. Tara stopped at the top of the steps and waited. The two were silent while Maggie mounted the steps to follow Tara into the grand foyer.

"Let me take a look at the room ya told me about," Maggie said as she dropped her belongings on the foyer floor and motioned for Tara to lead the way.

"There's nothing left untouched," Tara lamented as she led Maggie up the stairs and down the hall. "The curtains, the sofa, papers, broken glass... it's like a war was fought in there!"

As she swung open its door, she stopped, threw her hands over her mouth and stifled a cry. Maggie rushed past her and slowly took in the scene before her.

Neither woman spoke.

Maggie walked to the window, opened it, and tied back the draperies to allow as much air flow as possible. The sweet smell of summer permeated the room while a few moths rode the breeze and circled the lights. She found a screen leaning against the wall and positioned it in the window before turning to Tara with a puzzled look.

"I... I don't understand," Tara stammered in disbelief.

The warm, inviting glow of the desk lamp on the rich dark mahogany desk reflected the rays of light that bounced off the completely intact antique etched glass doors of the built-in bookcase that occupied the far wall. All of the books were in neat rows on the shelves. Her laptop rested in its usual place on her desk and ready for use. There was no sign of the chaos Tara spoke of.

"It happened. I'm not imagining things, Maggie. It happened!" Tara bellowed.

"Calm yourself lass. I'm not saying it didn't but there's no sign of it now. That's strange, wouldn't ya say?" Maggie mused as she gently pulled her book from the top shelf of the bookcase. Tara quietly watched Maggie slowly look through its pages until she found the section she wanted and held the book out for Tara to see the pages. "Is that what ya read?"

Tara moved next to Maggie. As she checked the pages a cold chill crept up her back. She stumbled away and fell onto the floor. When she looked up at Maggie the familiar form of her intruder -who she had determined was a ghost- was standing behind her. She reached out to point to him, but Maggie spoke before she could say anything.

"Never mind love, it isn't important," Maggie assured her as she reached to help her to her feet.

The old man stood motionless in the corner of the room watching the two women. A look of concern covered his face, but he said nothing. Tara struggled for footing as Maggie pulled her up from the floor. When she was once again steady on her feet she searched the room for the ghost but he was nowhere to be found.

"Maggie," Tara whispered.

"Yes?" Maggie replied.

"Did you see him?" Tara asked hesitantly.

"Who?" Maggie asked.

"Never mind," Tara said with a sigh.

She had no intention of giving more reason for Maggie to question her mind's stability.

FIVE

A week passed with nothing out of the ordinary occurring. Maggie cleansed the house and the surrounding property with herbs and incantations, insisting balance kept negative forces away. The old woman's presence in the house gave Tara a confidence and sense of security. There was something magical about her that was over and above what she demonstrated.

As they completed their daily meditation, Maggie reached for the bag she brought. She pulled out a small book. Its edges showed signs of usage and the binding was barely intact.

"Today we're going to talk about the powers of the mind," Maggie said.

"Do you mean maniesting?" Tara asked.

"Exactly," Maggie smiled, "making things happen by will. Knowing your abilities and making good use of them."

"It's so complicated," Tara said hesitantly. "I struggle so much with what you're teaching me, but I won't give up."

"The gift's inside ya already," Maggie said encouragingly. "Ya just have to pull it out. The day will come. Just keep learning and practicing and respecting what ya do not understand."

She moved close so Tara could see the writing on the pages of the book she held. "You're right about it being complicated. It takes a whole lifetime and then some to understand and then ya still have more to learn."

Maggie began reading from the book, "There is only one mind, and that's the mind of God. Some call it Spirit or Universal Intelligence, but it is God, the power of the mighty one. This mind is in all things on earth. God expresses through us, one and all. Everyone has the power of God running through them and everyone has the power of God to create, but this is only in accordance to what we believe, because we have free will to accept and reject. It's God's way to allow us this right. It's also God's way to allow us to use our powers for what we want." Maggie paused, watching for a sign that Tara was ready to hear more before continuing, "Man uses this power whether he realizes it or not. Learning to use it properly will give desired results." She positioned her body to face Tara. "Now, let's think of an example for a minute. If ya have a long beautiful sharp knife, ya can do good by using it to feed people or bad by killing someone with it but 'tis the same knife. Have ya got the picture in your mind?"

Tara nodded slowly and said, "Our decisions determine what happens?"

Maggie sat back with a satisfied sigh.

"I don't understand why God allows us to do harm with his tools," Tara mused. "He is all powerful so why doesn't he stop those doing harm?"

Maggie scowled for a brief moment and then replied, "If he stopped us from using the tools the way we choose we'd lose our free will. 'Tis a lesson in self-discipline and discernment of right and wrong."

"Does that go for spirits too?" Tara asked. "Do they have free will?"

Tara's mind raced with curiosity.

"They have the advantage of having a better idea of what 'tis all about, this life and thereafter. They do not have to be like us and pick the information through the human brain to boot!" Maggie replied thoughtfully.

"If that's true, then why are there bad spirits?" Tara persisted. "If they have an understanding about God and all the good there is available to them, why are they doing evil things? I don't understand."

"I asked the same thing myself at your age," Maggie said with a chuckle. "I'll give ya the same answer my mum gave to me. 'When ya leave your body in death, ya still have your mind with ya. Because ya still are under the right of free will, ya have the choice of believing ya should move into the light or not. That's why they send loved ones to get ya so you'll relax and believe better. Sometimes there's not a loved one to be found at your time and if ya don't have the faith to begin with, ya get scared, or angry or sometimes jealous that ya don't have your body anymore and ya wander the earth refusing to go on into the light. Sometimes ya meet up with others who are feeling the same way as ya are and ya form something like an army that joins the evil one to get back at those who still have what ya want. Lots of things could happen after ya die. That's why 'tis good to pray for the poor souls who have passed on, to help their energies be balanced and to let them see the truth and go back to God," Maggie paused and looked at Tara questioningly and then asked, "Does it make sense?"

"This makes perfect sense to me," Tara replied with a satisfied smile. "So much more sense than what I learned as a child."

"Good. Now let's get back to the making things happen part," Maggie said as she picked up the book and read, "Everything in life exists in thought first. If ya think about it hard enough, it can happen for ya. People do this, every day of their lives without understanding what they're doing. An example would be a man who believes he is a loser. He wants to be a winner, but deep down inside he feels he is a loser. Because of this he fails at life. If he changed his thinking of himself, he'd succeed."

"What about bringing money into your life, or a new love, or something like that?" Tara asked. "Would it happen just because you say it will?"

Maggie pursed her lips together and wrinkled her brow and said, "I guess the quickest answer is yes. Yes, as long as deep inside ya, that's what ya feel ya are worthy of and are ready for." Maggie tapped the side of her head, "Because it starts there, deep in the mind that's connected to God and then ya have to do what comes natural to help it happen. Like, get a good paying job or go to school or go out to meet people. Things like that."

"God helps those who help themselves," Tara beamed proudly.

"Indeed," Maggie agreed.

Tara wrinkled her brow and asked, "If it's all in the power of the mind, then why do people use candles and incense and rituals?"

"To help get the energies flowing in the right way so it will make it easier to happen and sometimes asking for help from the spirit side. Spirits respond to scents and words," Maggie explained.

"I see. What about all the blood sacrifices? Why them?" Tara persisted.

"Again", Maggie sighed as if getting bored with the conversation, "'Tis because some of these spirits are bad and they fool the people into believing that the only way they'll get what they're wanting is to do it that way. Remember, there's good and bad, greedy and generous on the spirit side too."

"This is all so fascinating!" Tara cried as she wiggled with excitement. Ignoring Maggie's obvious desire to move on she continued, "So the words in the book you gave me? The spirits respond to them?"

"Yep," Maggie said flatly.

"I learned when I was young that we have guardian angels and spirit guides," Tara said. "If that's true then why don't they stop the bad spirits from hurting us?"

"They can only help if we ask for their help. Otherwise they have to sit back and watch," Maggie sighed. "'Tis a pity."

Tara was thoughtful for a moment before asking, "The man I keep seeing in my dreams? Do you think he is my spirit guide?"

"I imagine so," Maggie replied.

"Maggie?" Tara spoke hesitantly, "If they can't help us

unless we ask for it, how do you explain all the times people get help from some mysterious source and then call them miracles? I mean, if they haven't asked for the help? Why are they being helped?"

"Ha," Maggie said with a chuckle. "Ya are full questions. Okay. Well, that's because in their dreams or in their subconscious, or maybe even before they were born they gave some kind of permission for certain kinds of help from their angels and their guides. To save their life maybe but not to give them easy street through life."

Tara placed her fingers to her temples.

"It's really deep," she said with a sigh. "I think I'll have to digest it a bit."

Maggie threw her head back in full bellied laughter and stood up. She walked to the bookcase and placed the little book on top of the large book she had already given Tara. Tara smiled, knowing this was the signal that this book was at her disposal to read whenever she felt the desire.

Maggie turned to Tara and stretched her arms back over her head as far as they would go and announced it was time to quit for the day.

"I agree," Tara said as she stood up and stretched. "It's about time for dinner. What do you feel like having?"

Tara did a mental survey of her kitchen cupboards while she waited for Maggie's response.

"Your birthday's soon, isn't it?" Maggie asked.

"In two days actually," Tara replied.

"You're eighteen, correct?" Maggie continued.

"That correct," Tara replied.

"That's as good an excuse as any to go to town for dinner," Maggie said with gusto.

"Oh! That's a fantastic idea," Tara said with genuine enthusiasm. "I haven't been out to eat since I moved here. Where should we go?"

Maggie smiled. She could never grow tired of Tara's youthful exuberance.

"Not too fancy," Maggie said. "I'm a simple woman." After a moment she added, "I know just the place for us."

****

It was good to be getting out amongst people. When she was in Manhattan, she used to dream of being able to get away from it all and be alone. Now, Tara dreamed of being in the middle of the masses again. She almost burst with anticipation as she pulled the car into the parking lot of the Great Pines Restaurant.

Maggie had guided Tara to an out of the way rustic restaurant, assuring her that, even though the surroundings were humble, the food was excellent. Tara didn't mind. She was happy to just be out socializing with a friend.

The wide planked floor creaked and groaned as they entered the dimly lit eatery that spoke of days gone by. While settling themselves at their table Tara spotted Brandon Wagner four tables away and froze, half-seated. He was playing with the food on his plate and didn't notice them. Tara couldn't help admiring the way his rich, dark hair reflected the glow of the candle that burned in the center of his table.

"Do ya know that fella?" Maggie asked quizzically.

"He's the one I told you about. The one I met that awful morning that everything happened. He has that enormous black gelding. We almost hit him with the car that day, remember?" Tara said.

She hoped she disguised the trembling response her body had at the sight of him.

"He's handsome," Maggie nodded in Brandon's direction.

Tara tried to subdue her embarrassment she said, "I guess."

"Ya like him just a bit, I think," Maggie teased.

Tara could feel her face going scarlet.

Taking pity on her friend, Maggie took the subject

away from Brandon and on to the history of the area. Tara listened earnestly.

Maggie was correct about the food. It was simple, but delicious. They were deciding upon dessert when Brandon approached them.

"You really should try the peach cobbler," he said in a rich masculine voice that sent delightful goose bumps up and down Tara's body. "It's delicious and the peaches are fresh this time of year."

Maggie assessed Brandon as he kept his steel grey eyes on Tara before bowing his head politely and leaving the restaurant. There was something about him that felt familiar but she couldn't quite place it.

Tara looked pale.

"Why does that man shake ya up so?" Maggie asked.

"I'm not sure. There's something about him that's unsettling. He stares at me as if he's looking inside me. Those eyes are, I don't know... familiar?" Tara said as she tried to hide her embarrassment. "It sounds crazy, right?" She refused to admit to Maggie or herself that not only was she unsettled by his eyes, but she was also embarrassed by the feelings that stirred within her whenever he was near. "You were staring at him in an odd way, Maggie. Your eyes got small and glassy."

"I was scanning his energy," Maggie explained.

"Do you mean his aura?" Tara asked.

"That's exactly what I mean," Maggie replied. "Ya can tell a lot about a person by the aura."

The topic of Brandon was dropped for the evening when the server came to take their dessert order and both women laughed as they simultaneously asked for the peach cobbler. They also requested a little brandy in their coffee to top off the meal.

Brandon was correct about the cobbler. It was the best Tara had ever tasted. She'd just finished the last of it when the server slipped a note to her. She opened it with both excitement and curiosity. Who would be sending her a note?

The only person she really knew in the area was sitting right across from her.

Tara's heart skipped a beat as she slowly read the bold handwriting.

I need to see you. Meet me at the clearing where we met tomorrow at 3:00 pm. Brandon.

Maggie made no mention of the note while she watched Tara stuff it nervously into her purse. She silently waited for Tara to speak.

Tara shifted uncomfortably in her seat as if debating what to do.

"When you were looking at his energy, what did you see?" she finally asked.

"His power," Maggie replied flatly.

"Power," Tara repeated. She was lost to Maggie's meaning.

Maggie took a sip of her coffee as if mulling over what to say next.

"There's a familiarity about him that I just can't place," she said.

"You too!" Tara exclaimed. She took a deep breath and pulled the note back out of her purse. "He wants to meet me tomorrow, but doesn't say why."

"Where? When?" Maggie asked as she leaned forward to look at the note.

"At the same spot where we met the other day at 3:00 tomorrow afternoon," Tara said softly.

Maggie frowned, "Are ya gonna do it?"

"I have to think about it," Tara replied.

"Maybe I'm old fashioned," Maggie mused, "but it seems to me if he wants to meet ya, he should meet ya in a nice restaurant or some other respectable place. Why in the middle of nowhere? It doesn't feel right to me."

"I'm curious," Tara said, "but you're right about him wanting to meet me in the middle of nowhere." After a moment of silence, she shrugged her shoulders and added, "I should pass."

"Smart lass," Maggie said. She smiled as she sat back in her chair and adjusted the napkin on her lap. "Your mama taught ya well."

Maggie and Tara simultaneously reached for the bill as the server placed it in the center of the table. Maggie was quicker and snatched it to her chest while she reminded Tara that the birthday girl shouldn't have to buy her own birthday dinner.

The evening air was warm and inviting as they stepped out of the restaurant. The two women decided to drive with the convertible top down so they could enjoy the beauty of the starry night. As they pulled out of the parking lot the moon cast shadows all around them. It was magical. Tara found herself discreetly searching for the earth fairies she'd read about as a little girl.

SIX

Since Brandon hadn't given Tara any information on how to contact him, she had no way of telling him she wasn't going to meet him. Feigning the need for a nap, she went to her room and paced. It was overwhelmingly tempting to go and see what he wanted, but she knew it wasn't the smartest thing to do. If he'd asked to meet her in the restaurant or even for a walk around town she might consider it, but not in the middle of nowhere.

The clicking of the clock on the recently refinished oak mantle echoed through the room as she continued to pace. She wanted to open the French doors leading to the small balcony attached to her bedroom but Maggie was in the lawn below, enjoying the afternoon sun and might realize she wasn't napping. She wasn't up to explaining her actions, nor could she explain them. It was as if an unknown and unseen force compelled her to go meet with this stranger and it took all of her will to ignore it.

The clock chimed three o'clock.

She wondered how long he'd wait before he realized she wasn't coming. It was an easy fifteen-minute ride on horseback to the spot where they'd met. Adding the time it took to tack up, it would take at least twenty-five minutes to get there. Even if she changed her mind and left now she doubted he'd still be there when she finally reached the spot. No one would wait twenty-five minutes, would they?

The nagging curiosity finally got the better of her. Tara made a feeble excuse about needing something at the store and Sugar needing the exercise and so it was a good idea to ride there to Maggie, who wondered if Tara really thought she bought the story. Thinking her foolish but not sensing any real danger from Brandon, Maggie shrugged her shoulders and returned to the book she enjoyed in the shade of an ancient gnarled apple tree.

Tara decided to forgo the saddle. Riding bareback wasn't something she was skilled at, but she could manage. She put the bit in Sugar's mouth and the mare tossed her head in anticipation and pawed the earth.

"Take it easy girl. You know I'm not good at this. Cooperate please!" Tara said as she climbed up onto the mounting stool.

As if she understood, the mare stood perfectly still.

While horse and rider headed in the direction of the designated meeting place, Sugar sensed Tara's growing urgency and broke into an easy lope down the well-trodden path through the woods. Tara's muscles synchronized with her mare. It was as if they were one. The fear she wouldn't be able to stay on without a saddle was replaced by exhilarated confidence. They were a team. They fit right. They felt right.

They reached the edge of the clearing with no sign of Brandon. Even though she hadn't expected him to wait for her, she was disappointed. Her disappointment changed to panic when she spotted his enormous black gelding bending over his limp body on the other side of the open field. She kicked Sugar into motion and flew to the ground before the mare completely stopped next to where he lay.

Brandon's face was buried in the tall grass. His breathing was labored, but steady. Pushing the enormous gelding out of her way, Tara rolled him onto his back and straightened his legs out. The wound on his head had started to clot. Although a fair amount of blood was all around his head, there was only a small amount of blood oozing from a fierce gash. She pulled the scarf off her neck and pressed it against his wound, wondering how long he'd been lying there. It must have been some time for the bleeding to slow down like it had.

The pressure of her hand made him wince even in his dazed state. She checked for more injuries and found a few cuts and bruises on his arms and back but was relieved there was sign of broken bones. The biggest worry was his head injury.

The gelding pranced nervously. She needed to quiet it down so she could somehow get Brandon on his back and find medical help. She held her breath and willed her heart to stop trying to clamber up her throat as she approached the intimidating beast.

"Can I help?" said a gentle, yet clearly masculine voice as it came up behind her.

After a brief startled jump, Tara forced enough composure within her to speak of the matter at hand.

"I found him like this. I'm not sure what to do," she said. "I already moved him a little. I know that's the wrong thing to do but his face was jammed in the ground and he had trouble breathing."

Thankful she was babbling to a real person and not some voice in the trees, Tara turned to face her newly arrived companion. She sucked in breath in awe. Never before had she come into contact with a more perfect looking man. The sun's rays flitted through his soft and refined golden hair as the light breeze tossed it whimsically about. Thick dark lashes that were the envy of every woman lined his deep brown eyes. Brilliant white teeth lined formed a neat row as he smiled and deep dimples on each cheek accentuated the strength of his chin. He stood tall and lean in a polo shirt and jeans, carrying himself like a model during a shoot; completely at ease and confident.

"I was out for a walk and saw you racing with the wind so I came to investigate. I'm Dominic," he said as he extended his hand to Tara. "You are..."

Tara quickly accepted Dominic's hand. "Tara. I'm Tara," she stammered, "and this is Brandon err... Wagner, Brandon Wagner." Her attention returned to the gravity of the situation. "I don't know what happened to him. I found him here like this. He needs a doctor."

"My wheels are parked on the other side of the clearing," Dominic volunteered. "Should I see if I can pull it over so we can get him loaded up and off to the hospital?"

Under normal circumstances, Tara would have found Dominic's comment of loading Brandon up as if he was a bale of hay offensive, but his overwhelming charisma had her so smitten it went right over her head. Without waiting for her response, he sauntered back across the clearing. She was about to ask him to hurry when a loud moan escaped Brandon's lips as he moved and made a feeble effort to sit up.

"Stay still," she urged. "You have a terrible gash on your head. Don't try to move until help returns."

"Who are you?" Brandon asked as he struggled to focus on Tara.

"I'm Tara. Don't you remember? You asked me to meet you here," Tara said, not sure whether she should be concerned or embarrassed.

"Tara. You came," he muttered.

His week smile gave him a boyish look as he settled back down, awaiting the help she'd promised.

It took some time for Dominic to come to the conclusion that he wasn't going to be able to maneuver his car across the clearing like he planned. There were too many ruts and hidden water patches. Before he found himself in serious trouble, he abandoned the idea and returned to Tara.

"I'm sorry but my car isn't going to make it over here. I can't risk getting it stuck," he apologized. He heaved a sigh, "I'm just going to have to carry him out."

Although Dominic appeared strong enough, Brandon was a few inches taller and practically dead weight. Tara mentally measured the distance this strange and handsome rescuer had to carry that dead weight and creased her brows.

"What about putting him on the back of his horse?" she asked,

"Good idea," Dominic said with relief. "Can you hold that beast steady for me?"

"I'll try," Tara replied as she took a deep breath to steady her nerves.

Dominic reached for the gelding's reins and handed them to Tara. Her heart pounded uncontrollably as she moved closer to the black beast. She had never been near so large and powerful a horse and his nervously wild actions made her apprehensive. To her relief and surprise, he stood in statuesque fashion while Dominic eased Brandon onto the saddle. He eased his lean, muscular body behind Brandon's limp one and held him steady while accepting the reins from Tara. She couldn't help admiring the way Dominic's muscular thighs strained against the fabric of his jeans as he positioned his feet in the stirrups. She stood back to get a better look at the picture they made. It reminded her of a western.

Dominic turned the gelding in the direction of the car and Tara searched for a log to help her climb back onto Sugar. "Leave it to me to ride without a saddle," she huffed. A large rock nearby offered just enough boost to help her on.

Dominic was halfway across the clearing by the time she caught up. Tara felt like she was riding a small pony next to them.

"My wheels are over there," he said as he nodded his head to the left.

Tara noticed a black Mercedes parked on the edge of the clearing. It was obviously the victim of traction trouble in the wet field. Bits of polished chrome glistened in the sunlight between clumps of mud. She fought the urge to giggle at the thought of Dominic attempting to drive a Mercedes across the clearing.

If Dominic noticed her amusement, he chose to ignore it. He asked her to hold the gelding while he slid to the ground and carefully lowered his limp burden. He half carried, half walked Brandon to the Mercedes and eased him into the back seat.

Tara noticed the blood was oozing more heavily from Brandon's wound.

She watched Dominic wipe a bit of blood from his hands after he closed Brandon in. She wondered how he could be so casual about someone bleeding in the back of his expensive car.

Tara couldn't help ogling as Dominic stretched his back before moving toward the driver's door. Realizing what she was doing, she looked away quickly to avoid the embarrassment of getting caught.

"I'm just passing through," he said. "Do you know where the nearest hospital is?"

"Yes, of course," Tara managed to say.

To her humiliation, she decided her admiration hadn't gone unnoticed when she saw his eyes twinkle with amusement.

"Maybe you should ride along to keep me from getting lost," he suggested.

"What about the horses?" Tara asked, grateful to take the attention away from her.

"I'll tend to them," Maggie said as she walked up next to a very surprised Tara and took the gelding's reins. She was already pulling Sugar behind her.

"Maggie? Where did you come from?" Tara asked with chagrin.

"I decided to stretch me legs and a good thing I did," she muttered as she looked long and hard at Dominic.

Tara assumed Maggie was also appreciating his good looks. After all, she was old not dead.

Dominic shifted uncomfortably under Maggie's inspection before regaining his composure.

"It's settled then," he said. "It's Tara, right? Let's get this poor fellow some medical care."

"Okay," Tara said as she mouthed her thanks to Maggie.

"Go on with ya," Maggie's face was like an emotionless mask, but her tone of voice was gentle and nurturing.

Tara rode in the back with Brandon to see if she could stop the bleeding with some pressure. As they drove along toward the hospital, she compared the two men. Both had beauty about them, but each in their own unique way. Brandon, with his tall, dark and handsome look that was compounded with a touch of mystery was in stark contrast to Dominic, who could only be described as a golden angel. He certainly was a gift from the heavens today. She didn't know what she would have done if he hadn't come along.

Dominic watched Tara tend to Brandon's wound in the rear-view mirror.

"Your friend took a nasty fall," he said.

"Yes," she agreed.

"Is he a close friend?" he asked.

"No," she replied with more emphasis than was necessary.

"No?" he mused.

"We've only just met, actually," she explained hesitantly.

"Hmm," he mumbled.

"What's meant by that?" Tara clipped.

She couldn't explain why she felt so irritated by his 'hmm', but she was. Perhaps it was his condescending tone?

"Nothing, really, it isn't my business," he said in a tone that bordered on smug. "I'm just making small talk, don't get upset."

Tara was upset. She knew how claiming she'd only just met this man -yet was meeting him in the middle of nowhere- looked. Brandon stirred and draped his arm over her slender legs. His hand slowly caressed her strong calf. She was going to remove it, but changed her mind. He was in a peaceful state so she saw no harm in allowing him this small liberty. He probably didn't even realize his actions. Plus, it actually felt soothing after such stress. Remembering she was the navigator, she turned her attention to the road and directed Dominic to turn left.

As they stopped at the emergency room entrance, Dominic asked Tara how Brandon was doing. She couldn't help responding to his handsome charm with a broad flirtatious smile. To her delight, he returned it with an equally dazzling one. For a brief moment, she forgot where they were and why they were there or that she was supposed to be embarrassed and irritated with him. Brandon's moans forced her back to reality. She gently removed his head from her lap as she slid out of the back seat. He raised his hands to his wound and groaned. It comforted Tara to see him coming around. He'd been in that dazed state for more than an hour. Tara wasn't a doctor, but she didn't think that was a good sign.

As Tara went for assistance, Dominic helped Brandon sit up. Brandon wailed in protest at the renewed pounding in his head the action caused.

"That's a nasty bump you have there. Do you remember how you got it?" Dominic asked while feigning concern.

"Ah," Brandon replied, "I'm not sure. Something hit my head. Aarrrggghhh! It hurts!" His vision hadn't fully returned so the twinkle in Dominic's eyes went unnoticed.

"I'll bet it does," Dominic mused while he tried to subdue a smile.

An attendant came out with a wheelchair and assisted Brandon into it. Tara went to registration and did her best to provide the information they required about a man she hardly knew. There was identification on him which helped and Brandon was able to speak enough to fill in the blanks. It felt like forever before the doctor was able to check Brandon and decide to keep him overnight for observation. His patient gave no argument.

Dominic insisted on driving Tara back to her home. He took advantage of the time alone by steering the conversation toward getting together for a drink. Tara delighted in the prospect and readily agreed. Dominic explained he had commitments elsewhere, but promised to look her up as soon as he was able.

Sugar raced alongside the Mercedes as it swung onto Tara's driveway. Tara watched him carefully as he ignored the horse and focused on her house and its surroundings. There was a glint of pleasure in them that was quickly masked with that aloof manner he'd been prone to display most of the afternoon.

"We just moved in a few months ago," she said defensively. "It's going to be lovely when I'm finished."

Tara didn't know why, but she wanted Dominic to admire her home as much as she did.

"It's a charmer now," he mused. "I was just admiring how peaceful and secluded it is. You must enjoy that. I know I would."

"I do," she said a little too quickly. Almost as fast as the words came out, the way they sounded registered in her mind. She'd insinuated to this perfect stranger that she lived alone out here in no man's land. Although she was alone at the moment, technically she lived with her father. "...err, we do," she added. Tara awkwardly grabbed door handle before adding, "I'm not alone. My father lives with me and Dennis is here on weekends so it isn't as peaceful as it might appear."

Dominic eyebrows rose quizzically.

"Dennis? For some reason I was under the impression you were unattached," he said softly.

"I am," Tara replied without hesitation.

She turned away blushing after her all too eager response and got out of the car.

The merriment swiftly left Dominic's face when he spotted Maggie coming across the lawn. She stopped briefly to speak to Tara and then continued on to him. As she approached she extended her hand. He reached through the window and took it hesitantly.

"Maggie's me name," she said boldly. "'Tis grand what ya did to help out and I thank ya."

Her eyes locked his unflinchingly.

He nodded his head in a slight acknowledgment while a look of concern flitted across his face before his casual amused look returned.

"It's a pleasure to meet you Maggie," he almost drawled. "I'm Dominic and I'm glad to have been of service."

Still locking eyes, Dominic slowly retrieved his hand from Maggie's solid grip and excused himself. He told her he had obligations to tend to. She smiled but kept her eyes locked on him. Shuddering visibly, he touched his brow lightly with his hand in a form of a salute and put the car in drive.

The old woman watched the Mercedes go around the circle near the house and down the drive toward the main road. She was still watching long after it disappeared.

SEVEN

The afternoon sun peaked through the tree tops as the cab weaved its way down the winding country lane toward Tara's house. Brandon took in the beauty of the old estate as he rolled down the window for a better look. The cool breeze felt good on his throbbing head. He raised his hand to the bandage the hospital secured before discharging him. It gave him the appearance of a battle worn soldier. The tender bump was reduced considerably but it still protruded out amongst the soft gauze.

He scowled. He had no recollection of how he was injured, no matter how hard he tried. He remembered waiting impatiently in the clearing for Tara. The next thing he remembered was waking up in the hospital with Tara next to him talking to a member of the hospital staff. As hard as he tried, he could recall no more. As the cab turned up the drive, he smiled to see his black gelding race through the paddock with Tara's chestnut mare at his heels. They made a beautiful sight. Their long silken manes and tails flowed with the movement of their powerful muscles. The reddish-orange hew of the setting sun as it peeked through the green foliage added to the scene.

At one point the half-mile long driveway edged the fence and the horses were side by side with the cab. The driver fell into competitive mode. He wore a devilish grin on his face as he laid his hand firmly on the horn and stepped on the accelerator. While the startled gelding jumped sideways in response, Sugar took on the challenge. She tossed her head high with nostrils flared while gathering her muscles for the push. Little did the cab driver know this was her favorite game. As they approached a precarious bend in the drive that led to the final stretch toward the house, he slammed on his brakes.

"There's a crater in the middle of this drive the size of a meteorite. The race is off. I can't believe I raced against a horse to begin with," the driver said, more to himself than to Brandon.

Brandon reached to steady his bandaged head as he jolted across the seat. His dark scowl looked menacing as he glowered at the driver. The driver guiltily cleared his throat as he watched Brandon through his rear-view mirror and somberly focused on easing the cab around the large pot holes in the drive. They finished the remaining distance in silence.

As they pulled up along the circular driveway in front of the house, Tara stepped out onto the porch. Brandon admired her slender silhouette in the dusky light. Her long hair fell in firelight wisps around her face and over her shoulders while her sun baked skin gleamed against a white gauze peasant dress, exposing just enough flesh to make him want to see a little more.

Tara felt uncomfortable under his intense stare and quickly averted her eyes. She tugged at the bodice of her dress in an attempt to cover her burning flesh.

"I'm glad to see you found the place okay," Tara blurted out in an attempt to camouflage her uneasiness.

"It was a beautiful drive out here. You're fortunate to have such beauty available to you on a daily basis," Brandon drawled as he eased out of the cab. His injury required moving cautiously. As he leaned in to pay the cab, Tara struggled unsuccessfully to hear their brief, muffled conversation. When Brandon moved away from the he cab and it drove off, she stood in puzzlement.

Brandon looked amused as he asked, "Is something wrong?"

"Well, uh... he left... without you," she stammered.

She blushed at the obvious panic in her voice. The thought of being alone together made her shiver with excited anticipation that she desperately tried to hide.

"I can hardly fit my horse in the back seat," Brandon said with a broad grin that displayed a set of strong white teeth. "I want to thank you for keeping him here for me."

"It was no problem at all. Sugar loved the company," she said a little too quickly.

"Sugar?" he asked.

Tara grinned apologetically.

"My mare," she explained.

"That's right, your mare." Brandon chuckled, "I thought you had someone else here with you."

"I do," she said quickly.

Her excitement at being alone with this man turned to nervousness. After all, she really didn't know him. She quickly turned away and busied herself picking up some empty clay pots that she left on the porch earlier after transplanting the flowers into the window boxes along the front and side of the house. Now she would be expected to produce a companion of some sort and there was no one.

Concerned that she would be found out, she changed the subject.

"What do you call your horse?" she asked in as steady a voice as she could muster.

"King," he replied. Not to be swayed from the topic of her living conditions he continued, "You said you have a companion living here? For some reason I thought you were single."

"Do you plan on riding King home tonight? Is that wise?" she asked, deliberately ignoring his question about her singleness.

"I don't know how wise it is," he replied casually, "but the old boy is a devil when it comes to trailers so I think it might be the lesser of the two evils."

Tara caught her breath as Brandon flashed his seductive smile her way.

"There ya are. I looked for ya for a while now," Maggie

said as she stuck her hand out to shake Brandon's in a not too gentle manner. "Is it the man I last saw lying all bloodied up in the grass?"

Although grateful for her presence, Tara found herself speechless. Maggie had moved home that afternoon and she hadn't heard her return.

"I heard ya speaking so I thought I'd check to see who the company was," Maggie continued. "I'm not intruding am I?"

Brandon flinched under the jolt of Maggie's handshake. He smiled weakly while politely stating his pleasure in finding her there. Neither Tara nor Maggie was certain he meant it.

Tara was grateful Maggie showed up since it backed up her story of not being alone. She invited everyone to join her on the back patio. She'd developed the habit of admiring the moon in the early evenings with a glass of wine or a cup of tea, depending on her mood and her company. Brandon eagerly joined her, but Maggie declined. She had only returned to retrieve a few things she left behind that afternoon and needed to get back to Angus. Disappointed, Tara watched Maggie go into the house. She turned to Brandon who stood quietly watching her. Her heart beat against her chest so hard that she was sure he could see it. Taking a deep breath, she walked past him toward the back part of the porch, suddenly eager for that wine.

"Are you old enough to drink?" Brandon asked, after noticing how her hands where fumbling with the bottle.

"In my own home, yes... in a restaurant... it depends upon the state I'm in," she replied nervously.

"Shall I pour?" he asked quietly.

"I can't seem to get it together! It's been that way all day," she lied.

She hated lying but she didn't know what else to say to cover the nervousness that permeated her whole being. Handing the bottle to Brandon, she walked over to the railing and tilted her face toward the sky.

"The moon's so beautiful," she mused. "When I was a little girl I used to look for the man in the moon. I thought how lucky he was to be living on such a big bright ball and be able to watch over at the stars like that. Did you believe in the man in the moon?"

"I still do," Brandon said with a chuckle as he handed her a glass of wine and raised his to a toast.

"In some ways I do too," Tara said.

She touched her glass to his and drank eagerly. The sweet nectar was smooth and soothing. Within moments she felt calmer and more relaxed.

"Do you ride King often in the moonlight?" she asked with concern.

"Never," he replied.

"This is your first attempt... with an injury like that?" she exclaimed.

"There's a first time for everything, right?" he said with a shrug.

Brandon kept his tone light, but he questioned the wisdom of riding King in his condition, let alone in the dark. He would have liked to wait a few more days for his head to heal more, but he didn't want to saddle Tara with the imposition of King's care. He wanted to be in good standing with her.

"Do you think that's wise?" Tara asked with genuine concern.

"I'm not really sure how wise it is," he said softly, "but it seems like my only choice. It's a shame they released me so late today. I would have preferred to ride in the daylight."

"How long a ride is it?" she asked hesitantly.

"I'm not really sure," he said. "I think I should stay on the roadside since King's not as brave as he looks and the woods can be confusing. So, no short cuts." He thought for a moment while absent-mindedly fondling his bandage. "I've never traveled on the road to the boarding stable but I'm guessing it's probably close to an hour's ride."

Tara looked past him into the grove and sucked in her

breath.

He turned to follow her stare and stepped back when he saw the creature creeping up on them; its teeth were bared menacingly. Brandon squeezed his eyes shut a few times to make sure he wasn't seeing things. He had just endured a nasty injury, after all. As hard as he tried he couldn't make the beast disappear. It had the head of a vicious wolf but its body resembled a mountain lion. He put his glass on the patio table with slow deliberation and stood in front of Tara.

"Move away slowly, Tara," he said in a soft and steady tone. "Move slow and steady into the house. Go now."

Tara followed Brandon's instructions while he stood firmly in place, not certain what he should do next. The creature was too close for him to make a run for it. He looked around for something within easy reach to use as a weapon.

Once inside, Tara rushed to find Maggie. Gasping for air, she babbled about the creature Brandon faced outside. Maggie pulled a pistol from her bag and rushed to see for herself. Positioning herself not far from Brandon she held the pistol at arm's length and closed one eye to focus before shooting the beast. It exploded on impact. Body shards disappeared into nothingness.

Tara stared at the space the beast stood in only moments before.

"What was that?" Tara asked hesitantly.

"A demon creature," Maggie replied. "There are probably more where it came from but I doubt they'll bother us tonight. Even so, we shouldn't try to go anywhere. 'Tis better to be safe than sorry, right?" She turned to address Brandon. "Better get the horses tucked away. Those demons love flesh."

The uneasiness Tara experienced when Maggie suggested Brandon stay quickly switched to horror at the thought of another creature like the one she just saw explode getting to the horses. She raced past Maggie and Brandon toward the paddock with Brandon not far behind. Sugar and King were prancing in the moonlight.

Even in the state of panic, Tara admired their beauty. King was a full hand taller than Sugar and much wider. His thick neck arched and he held his tail high while he pranced around her in a seductive dance of nature. Sugar reared on her hind quarters; twisting and hopping in the dance of the wild. When Tara called out the two ceased their display and raced to the fence. Brandon watched with surprise as the two animals followed Tara into the barn. She used no leads or any other means of assistance. She simply told them to follow her and they did. He'd never seen his gelding this complaisant. It was an amazing sight.

The glow of the full moon silhouetted the trio as they made their way into the barn. Brandon turned his head toward the tree line where he'd seen the wolf creature. All seemed calm.

"Keeping your eyes open, eh? 'Tis a good idea, I know I said they probably won't bother us tonight, but in truth I don't think we've seen the last of them," Maggie whispered behind Brandon. "She's a bit skittish as it is. Let's be on the look out and say nothing, deal?"

"Deal," Brandon said as he did his best to hide his disconcertment with Maggie's ability to sneak up on people.

"What's a deal?" Tara asked as she walked up quietly behind them.

Brandon and Maggie turned to her as Maggie answered quickly, "He's agreed to let me have a go at that black giant tomorrow before he leaves. He's a mighty beast that one!"

"Why Maggie, I didn't know you ride," Tara said with surprise. "You can ride Sugar any time you want."

"'Tis more the thrill of conquering such a mighty beast than the ride," Maggie said and laughed boisterously to lighten the mood. Well, I need me sleep. I sure hope Angus will be okay without me. He's pretty dependent ya know, but it can't be helped. I'll see ya both in the morning."

"Good night" Tara and Brandon said simultaneously.

"Sweet dreams" Tara added. Stretching in a cat-like manner, she moved away from Brandon and walked toward the house. "I know it's early, but I'm beat too," she called back to him. "I hope you don't mind. If you'll follow me I'll show you to your room but, please, you're welcome to stay up as long as you like. If you're hungry, there's some fruit in a bowl on the counter and some chicken in the refrigerator or you can look for something else. Please make yourself at home. Mi casa su casa."

"I appreciate your hospitality," Brandon said stiffly. "Thank you, miss."

His formality took Tara by surprise.

"Please call me Tara," she almost whispered.

She was so confused right now. She wanted to get to know Brandon but wanted to stay distanced from him at the same time. She never felt the way she felt in his company and she wasn't sure how to deal with it; hence the reason to keep her distance. Those, compiled with the events of the evening made her want to crawl beneath the safety of her bed coverings.

"Call me Brandon," he said as he walked a little too close.

She quickly stepped away and studied him. The moonlight cast an eerie glow to add to the mood of the evening. Shadows played with his dark hair and steel grey eyes, giving his handsome looks a sinister edge.

"I will," Tara said.

She wasn't sure if the shiver up her spine was from the excitement she felt whenever he was close or from the power the combination of the moonlight and the dark mood of the evening gave him.

They walked in silence into the house and he followed her up the staircase to the second floor.

"Your room is just down the hall," she said.

When she realized Brandon was no longer right behind her but standing at the foot of a narrow flight of steps that led to the third floor, she stopped short and waited.

"What's up there?" he asked as he moved closer to the stairwell and peered past the gate she put up to keep the animals from going up it.

"I keep it blocked off until I'm able to work on it. This house is quite large for one person," she said matter-of-factly.

"You mean two, don't you?" Brandon inquired "You and Maggie? I'm a little confused because she said she only stopped by for some things, but you stated you weren't here alone and she's the only person I've seen."

"My father lives with me but is traveling right now, my brother comes on weekends, and Maggie comes and goes as she pleases," she explained as she resumed her lead to the room Brandon was to occupy.

The room she decided to place him in was near the room Maggie claimed. When she reached the door, she opened it and told him to make himself comfortable before quickly excusing herself.

The walk to her own room felt eternal. She sensed his eyes boring in her back. She'd deliberately placed Brandon in a room as far away from hers as possible. Even so, she locked her door and placed a chair in front of it before she was comfortable enough to sleep.

As she lay dozing off, Tara contemplated on the real reason for her actions. Was it to keep him out, or to keep her in?

EIGHT

Beams of moonlight trickled through the shutters that Brandon threw open. He lifted the window to let in the night air. From the staleness of the room, he could tell that it was closed up for quite some time. He stood in the dark and watched moonlit shadows dancing across the furnishings.

He had a sense of not being alone. The hair on the back of his neck was on end and a shiver ran up his spine. He wondered if it was such a good idea to stay after all. Things were different. He felt a change about the property as soon as he got out of the cab. It was a feeling he hadn't felt in a long time; a sense of danger, but of what? He sensed it was more than the evil looking creature Maggie killed, although he couldn't quite put his finger on it.

A soft scratching on his door caught his attention. With graceful, silent strides he made his way from the window to the door and paused with his ear to the wood. There was a small thud and then more light scratching. He eased the door open. Maggie stood motionless, holding one finger to her lips, while beckoning him to follow with another.

Brandon eased his tall frame out into the hallway and followed her to the servant's stairwell. The stairs moaned under their weight and they stopped several times to listen for signs of Tara stirring. Although he had no clue what she was up to, he sensed it was best to keep Tara out of it.

Maggie led him to the study that was dimly illuminated by a few tapered candles and poured them both a brandy. As he reached out to take it from her bony, well used hand their eyes locked. He felt a familiarity about her. A good majority of his memories were still all jumbled from his accident but he was certain they would return eventually and then he'd know why he felt like they already knew each other.

"I feel like we know each other too," she said softly. "Yet for the life of me I don't know why."

He stepped back, completely thrown off by her display of abilities. Brandon held his glass to his lips while watching her warily, barely sipping it.

Are you some kind of a witch or something?" he finally asked.

"Witch? That's what you're calling me? Witch?" Maggie hissed as she stood glowering at Brandon with her hands on her hips, her legs spread apart, and a large scowl on her face. If she had a parrot on her shoulder and a patch on her eye, she would have easily passed for a pirate; an offended one at that.

"I meant no offense. I'm sorry. I didn't know you would react like that. You read my mind and I tried to figure out why. I apologize," he said with sincerity as he stepped away from the light of the moon.

"Quite a player, aren't ya?" she spat.

His apology hadn't soothed the tone in her voice.

"Player?" he said with confusion.

Brandon was either a good liar or he really didn't know what Maggie was referring to. She scowled with frustration. It was rare for her to not be able to know if someone was good or bad, but with the last two men who came around Tara she'd had a dickens of a time. She shook her head in hopes of clearing away whatever blocked her.

"Never mind," she said. "We don't have time for this. Just remember I'm watching ya." She tossed back a decent amount of brandy. "Witch indeed."

Maggie put the candle down on the mantelpiece and moved to sit on the end of the sofa. After lighting a small hurricane lamp on the center of the coffee table, she opened the family book she placed there earlier and leafed through the pages.

"Can I ask why we are using candles instead of the

lights? Is there something wrong with the electricity?" he asked as he positioned himself in a chair not far from her.

"I don't want to be too noticeable," she replied in a tone that was short and crisp.

"Oh, okay," he said.

He was clearly perplexed as he relaxed back into the chair. The woman obviously was a little off her rocker, but she seemed harmless enough.

"Can I ask what we are doing?" he asked.

"No" she answered without raising her eyes from the pages.

She found what she was looking for and was running her fingers under the words as she read them.

Brandon smiled with amusement while he watched her lips silently forming each syllable.

"Well, can I ask then why I'm here if I'm not to know what we are doing?" he persisted.

"Quiet!" she snapped.

Still not looking up, Maggie briskly and flatly made it clear to Brandon that he was to speak no more.

Taken aback by her outburst, he sat back quietly. The ticking of the large grandfather clock in the corner of the room echoed in the silence. Its rhythm mesmerized him into a trance like state. He slowly relaxed as he finished his brandy and set the glass on the table next to him. His impatience leaving him, he stretched his legs as far in front of him as they would go and sank even deeper into the chair. Exhausted from the exertion of his first day out of the hospital, he fell into a deep sleep.

Maggie lifted her eyes at Brandon only after she was satisfied that he was in a deep slumber. She'd deliberately ignored him while he drank the special tonic she placed in his brandy. She expected its effects to last until the morning but she decided to be quick, just in case. She hadn't made that recipe in years and wasn't sure about the strength of the dosage. Closing the book, she walked over to the window and pulled back the drapes. The moon glowed like a brilliant flashlight, illuminating the grounds and making it easy for her to see the world outside. She searched for more demon creatures, but all looked quiet. This was good. Maybe there would be no more attacks.

Even though it was unlikely, she could hope.

She walked over to Brandon and rolled up his sleeve. Picking up the black bag she tucked into recesses of the closet of the room she claimed as hers during her overnight visits she reached in and pulled out a syringe, cotton swab, alcohol and thin scarf. She set them all neatly on the table next to his chair and then pulled out two small amber colored bottles. She opened the tops of each bottle and set them down next to her supplies.

Howling pierced the night.

"Not now!" She moaned.

This was poor timing. Reaching in her black bag, she pulled out the pistol that only hours before had served her so well. Pulling her body up to full height, she took a deep breath and walked to the front door. She stepped out onto the porch and with no time to spare shot the pistol directly into the chest of a leaping demon creature. If she'd hesitated for a mere five seconds longer, it would have reached her. The beast exploded and disappeared. She spun to the left and shot again; grazing another beast, but not killing it. The wounded creature yelped and lunged for her. Maggie shot again and this time hit her mark. Two more came toward her from seemingly nowhere. She took a deep breath and shot the one on the left first and then the one on the right; watching them both explode with determined satisfaction.

Silence prickled the air as the old woman waited for more. Her chest heaved, her heart beat wildly, and adrenaline raced through her veins. When five minutes passed and she still saw nothing, she lowered the pistol and returned to the parlor.

Brandon slept peacefully in the chair, completely unaware of what just transpired. She listened nervously for signs of Tara awakening but all was quiet. She poured herself more brandy and downed it quickly before returning to Brandon's side. With rapid agility she wrapped the thin scarf around his upper arm and hunted for a suitable vein. When she as satisfied she'd located the best spot, she wiped his skin with an alcohol swab and inserted the needle. Blood flowed smoothly into the syringe while she loosened the scarf. When the syringe was full, she removed the needle and placed pressure over the tiny puncture. Gently laying the syringe of blood on the table, she wiped his arm clean and lowered his sleeve.

Maggie picked up the syringe and slowly dispersed its contents equally into the two amber bottles. Once done, she recapped the bottles and put everything back into her black bag.

Brandon stirred slightly and she guessed he wouldn't be under much longer. Either he was quite powerful or she'd omitted something from the potion. Shaking her head at the situation, she extinguished the hurricane lamp, picked up the candle and left the room.

****

Tara stopped at the top of the stairs and stared down the hall at the door of Brandon's room. She wondered how he'd slept. Her night was fitful. The moon's bright rays managed to creep past her closed drapes and illuminate her room. When she did manage to sleep she kept reliving that awful wolf-creature snarling at them from the edge of the grove.

In the confusion, she hadn't had a chance to ask Maggie if she knew where it came from. She was sure it was a breed of wild animal that must have strayed from its den deep in the woods. There was one thousand acres of state land just beyond her property which was plenty of space for creatures to live in undetected. The vision of it bursting under the impact of Maggie's shot kept popping into her head and she heard the shots over and over again in her sleep. Her first thought upon awakening was the mess it must have left and the chore of cleaning it up. Country life and nature still made her queasy at times.

Tara stopped at Maggie's bedroom and found she already rose and left. So much for her riding King. She learned early on to take her friend as she was. Her lack of predictability was part of her charm.

As she approached Brandon's door, she wished she had the courage to look in. She longed to see his sleeping face. Was it still as disarming as when he was awake and alert or did it soften and become more child-like? Uneasiness flowed through her abdomen as she thought about his sleeping body just beyond the thick mahogany door. She remembered the tightness of his form under his free-flowing clothes when he stepped out of the cab and the feel of him as she cradled him in the back of the Mercedes enroute to the hospital. His body was hard and strong. Shaking the thoughts from her head, she made for the servant's stairs that led to the kitchen.

A gasp of surprise escaped her when she entered the kitchen and discovered her house guest at the table drinking a mug of coffee. His smile was as disarming as ever. When he raised his mug in her direction, she struggled to maintain composure.

"Good morning. I hope it's okay. I was desperate for a cup of coffee. My head is in one major fog this morning," Brandon said as he stood up and walked over to the cupboard. "Can I get you a cup?"

As he turned his head to look at her he winced and raised his hand to his bandage.

Tara looked at him thoughtfully.

"Are you sure it's wise to ride King today?" she asked. "You only turned your head to look at me and winced. Do you think you'll be able to handle an hour in the saddle?"

Brandon paused thoughtfully.

"Truthfully I'm not sure," he admitted, "but I do not want to overstay my welcome, nor do I want to take advantage of your good nature. Not to mention the fact that my project has been neglected for some time now."

It hadn't dawned on Tara that Brandon had a life outside of her reality.

"Work," she mused. "I didn't think about that. What do you do?"

"I...I'm a photographer," he stammered through his lie.

"Freelance or corporate?" she asked, thinking he stammered because he was embarrassed and wanting to assure him she found photography interesting.

"Freelance. I'm here on multiple assignments for... magazines," he explained with hesitancy. "I've taken photos of these beautiful hills and their wildlife for some time now."

The mention of wildlife reminded her of the night before. Her stomach twisted as she walked over to the coffee pot, picked up the cup he set out for her, and she poured herself some of the steaming onyx liquid.

"Are you hungry?" she asked.

She was anxious to change the subject since he clearly didn't want to talk about his work.

"I thought about your offer for me to make myself at home last night," he smiled wistfully. "If you had come down just a few minutes later, you would have found me whipping up an omelet."

"I can handle an omelet," she offered. "You take it easy and then I'll drive you wherever you need to go. King is fine where he is for now."

There was a long silence while the two exchanged looks, each one trying to determine the other's thoughts. There was something about this man that intrigued her, yet left her feeling unsettled. His eyes were alluring and his smile irresistible. Feeling her cheeks flush, Tara turned back to the coffee pot.

"I appreciate that," he finally said softly.

The two jumped simultaneously as footsteps sounded

in the dining room and then laughed. They were still smiling when Dennis entered the room. He looked at Brandon and raised an eyebrow in Tara's direction.

"Am I interrupting?" he asked with a tense face and a curt smile.

"Not at all," she gushed, knowing full well how it must look to her brother. "This is Brandon..."

"Wagner," Brandon finished Tara's introduction as he stood to shake Dennis' hand, "and you are?"

"Her brother," Dennis said with a scowl, "who she obviously forgot was coming this morning."

Dennis and Brandon turned to Tara as she set her cup down on the counter just a little harder than necessary.

"I didn't forget you were coming," she snapped. "What are you insinuating?"

"Nothing," Dennis said. "It's perfectly natural to come here at seven in the morning to find you entertaining a strange man over coffee. I'm not insinuating a thing." Dennis' voice sounded strained as he moved closer to Tara.

"Whoa! Calm down buddy. This isn't at all what you think," Brandon said with an equally strained voice.

"It's Dennis," Dennis growled.

His face was clearly contorted with possessive jealousy, mixed with concern and worry over his sister's tendency to be too trusting and naive.

In Brandon's attempt to calm Dennis down, he'd forgotten about his condition and moved too quickly. His head throbbed so badly he couldn't stop himself from holding it.

"What's wrong with him?" Dennis asked with genuine concern as he watched Brandon cradle his bandaged head in his hands.

"He's the man who was hurt in the field the other day. He came by yesterday to get his horse," Tara said defensively.

She was irritated by her brother's actions but not surprised. He was fiercely protective of her and still not comfortable about her being so far from civilization alone. Finding a strange man in the kitchen at that hour of the morning would raise the hair on anyone's neck. "Maggie stayed the night but she left before I got up."

"So, you had a regular slumber party, eh?" Dennis mused. His tone was noticeably softened. Knowing Maggie was there during the night was all the reassurance he needed. "Sorry I couldn't make it."

"Well, it wasn't planned, I assure you," Tara said. "Maggie insisted we all stay put because there was some kind of weird looking wolf in the grove last night. She killed it, but she was worried there might be more. She insisted everyone wait until daylight to venture back out. I haven't a clue what time she left."

"I woke up at six o'clock and she was already gone," Brandon volunteered as he walked to the coffee maker and poured himself another cup. His stomach rumbled so loud he looked at Tara with a mixture of amusement and embarrassment.

Tara smiled and started pulling the makings of an omelet out of the refrigerator.

"I think that's my cue to start cooking," she said. "Are you hungry Dennis? We're having omelets."

"It sounds good but I ate on the way out here," Dennis replied while rubbing his stomach for emphasis. I think I'll just start painting dad's room. I thought it would be nice to have it finished when he returns. Join me when you can, okay sis?"

Dennis gave Brandon a curt nod before he kissed Tara's cheek and left the room.

"Please excuse my brother," she said softly after Dennis was clear from earshot. "He's a bit over protective but he means no harm. Once he gets to know you he's your best friend."

"I don't blame him," Brandon said. "I think I might be the same way."

His bold look left no mystery to his meaning. She couldn't control the heat rising in her cheeks. A shell fell into the bowl while she fumbled with the eggs.

"Darn it!" she exclaimed.

"Can I help?" Brandon asked.

"Well, as long as you're up you can set up the table. There's orange juice in the refrigerator and can you start the toast?" she said thoughtfully. "The toaster is by the bread box. Oh, there's a new jar of jam in the pantry; raspberry I think. Can you get that out as well? I think the one in the refrigerator is so low it won't be enough. I hope I took the butter out of the freezer! Will you check?"

"Do you want me to make the omelet too?" he joked.

Brandon's broad smile lit up the room as he went about doing her bidding. In her nervousness, his joking remark went right over her head. She simply declined and kept working.

They ate breakfast in relative silence. Tara was pre-occupied with her own nervousness and confusion and Bran-don's pounding head consumed his attention. He felt a mi-graine brewing.

She broke the silence just as he washed his last bite of breakfast down with juice.

"I need to help my brother for a while," she said apolo-getically. "You look like your head is hurting. Maybe you would like to lie down for a while. I shouldn't be more than a few hours."

"That sounds like a plan," he said. "I could use just a bit more rest."

"I'm so sorry..." she started.

Brandon quickly interrupted her.

"It's nothing with the house," he assured her. "It's my head." He decided not to mention his slumber in the chair after his rendezvous with Maggie. He wasn't really lying. His head maintained a constant dull ache. "The accommodations are perfect. It's just this," he said as he pointed to the bandage.

"Can I ask where you're staying?" Tara asked while taking the liberty to lightly lift the bandage and peek under it.

He leaned forward to make her ministering easier.

"At the motel down the road," Brandon responded, wincing involuntarily when she pulled too hard on the bandage.

"You, poor man," she said sympathetically as she released the bandage and started cleaning up the kitchen. "Maybe you should just stay here for a few days. I mean, you don't have any one to really care for you at the motel and I don't think it's a wise idea to try to travel with that head. You should be fine in a few days."

She couldn't believe her own words. Was she volunteering to take care of this man she could hardly keep her eyes -let alone hands- off until he healed up? Was she mad?

"I appreciate the offer, but I do not wish to impose," he drawled lazily as he stood up to help her with the dishes.

Relief, mixed with regret, flooded Tara. Thankful that the temptation of having him so close and being vulnerable to his charms was removed, she also regretted not having more time alone with him in the intimate setting a sick bed would provide.

"It's your call," she said softly. "Tell you what. Why don't you go lay down for a while and we'll see how you feel later today and make our decision then? Sound good?"

"Sounds good," he smiled warmly.

She wasn't sure if she should be flattered or concerned by the way his steel gray eyes consumed her. This man was definitely an unreadable mystery. He turned quietly and left the room. She finished the dishes and went to join Dennis.

****

As soon as Brandon entered the room he'd occupied the night before he caught a flash in the corner of his eye. He turned to get full view, but it was gone. It happened so suddenly he wasn't even certain how big it was, but he was sure there was something. He cautiously opened doors, looked behind furniture and moved the drapery away from the window and found it was closed. Disappointed and tired he collapsed onto the bed and was fast asleep in moments.

The sun inched its way behind the mountain tops by the time he awoke. Shadows danced around the room from the trees outside his window, indicating it was early afternoon. It took him a few minutes to get his bearings straight and remember where he was. As he sat on the edge of the bed, he spotted his reflection in the mirror. His thick black hair was in disarray, dark whiskers sported his face and his shirt was rumpled from sleeping in it. As he ran his tongue across his teeth, the thick film that formed while he was sleeping made him shudder.

He definitely needed to clean up.

He headed to the bathroom across the hall. Its faded flowered wallpaper gave the impression of being the original, but he knew better. The small lines and cracks dispersed throughout the paper accentuated its charm. A large claw footed bathtub dominated the room. The toilet was as old as the house with the water tank positioned high on the wall and a pull chain for flushing. The large crack in the ornate pedestal sink made him think the slightest bit of pressure would split the bowl in half. It was clear it wasn't a main bathroom but it was functional and spotlessly cleaned.

He searched the medicine cabinet on the wall and was pleased to find shaving supplies and a few new toothbrushes. A broad smile spread across his face as he gingerly removed his clothes. His complements went to Tara for her thoughtful preparedness.

He admired how brightly polished the brass knobs of the faucet were as he filled the squeaky clean, oversized, claw-footed tub with steaming hot water. There was a bottle of bubble bath sitting on the shelf near the tub. It was when he reached for it that he noticed his arm. He stood motionless, hanging over the tub with the bubble bath in his hand as he stared at a bruise, about the size of a silver dollar on the inside of his elbow. It was as if someone had drawn his blood, and done a sloppy job of it at that! He scrutinized where the hospital staff pricked and poked but their ministries were clean and well done. This wasn't from the hospital. He went over the previous night in his mind but there was no time that he could remember where he'd been in a situation to injure his arm like that. It was a mystery.

He slowly poured the liquid soap under the running water and swirled the bubbles to disperse them along the water's surface. His head felt like his brain was playing racket ball against his skull. The strain of trying to remember the night before brought the pounding back full force. He decided to try to figure it out later and just relax for a while. Lowering himself as far as he could into the deep tub, he reveled in the feel of the warm bubbles all around him. It was a long time since he soaked in a bath and three days since he'd even showered! The hospital insisted on a wash down from the ugliest nurse they could recruit because they didn't want his head to get wet and the wound wasn't in a place where a shower cap could protect it. The water was soothing and comforting.

He reached for a wash cloth and drenched it with the warm soapy water. Pulling his bandage gently from his head with one hand, he dribbled the warm liquid over it with the other, creating shivers of pleasure down his spine. Not certain how his head would respond, he slowly immersed himself until only the wound was above water. All of the muscles in his body relaxed and he felt completely relaxed for the first time in days.

Eventually the water grew tepid and he forced himself to climb out of the tub. The gurgling of the draining water, mixed with his humming, echoed off the walls. He stood naked while he leaned into the mirror that hung over the pedestal sink and inspected his head wound. It was long and ugly with a considerable number of stitches. The doctor assured him that it would heal with little, if any, scar but he wondered about the accuracy in that statement.

He pulled the shaving supplies and a toothbrush from

the cabinet but found no toothpaste. He shrugged and set out tackling his whiskers. The scraping sound of the razor against his brittle whiskers sounded abnormally loud. It made him uncomfortable and so he opened the water faucet to drown the sound with running water. A cool breeze swept across his back and he turned to see if the door had popped open, but it was secure. The window was closed as well.

Spotting a large crack in the corner wall he made a mental note to mention it to Tara. He was sure she planned to get around to this part of the house eventually but the breeze was strong which indicated a rather large leak. She would have to take care of it before the cold weather set in, whether it was on the top of her 'to do' list or not.

With his shaving completed, he rummaged deeper into the recesses of the cupboards for toothpaste. He finally found a small travel size tube and went to work on the thick film that accumulated over the last twenty-four hours.

Brandon had a habit of remaining naked after a shower or bath for a few minutes before dressing. It was a habit his mother instilled in him with her old-world belief that the body needed time to breathe before smothering it with clothes for long hours at a time. He peeked cautiously out the door down the hall to make sure it was empty. His lean, muscular -and very naked- body filled the doorway as he stepped through it and into the hall. A loud gasp reached his ears that stopped him in his tracks. Tara stood at the top of the servant's stairs. Neither one knew what to do next. She cleared her throat with gusto, breaking the stillness, and he quickly shifted his body to camouflage as much as possible; not as much for his sake as for hers. She was as embarrassed as a schoolgirl.

"Ex... excuse me. I was just..." she stammered.

"I'm sorry I thought I was alone upstairs. Forgive me," he said with an apologetic tone that was in contrast with the mischievous twinkle in his eye.

"No... No prob... No problem. I'll just... go down to my room. Sorry," she stammered as she scurried off to her room without waiting for a response from him.

Brandon could tell by the look in her eyes that she may have been shocked but she was also intrigued. He heaved a heavy sigh as she disappeared into her bedroom. It wasn't planned, but he'd hoped the shock of seeing him naked would jog her memory.

****

Tara leaned against her bedroom door. Her heart beat against her eardrums as she tried to calm her trembling legs. The surprise of seeing Brandon standing nude in her hallway in the middle of the afternoon was enough to shake her to the core, but it was more than that. There was a familiarity and longing mixed with her shock. She couldn't identify what was happening to her. It left her feeling hollow and unsettled and she couldn't understand it. What was it about him that made her blush like a schoolgirl as well as tremble like a prey avoiding a predator? One thing she knew for certain was that she wanted to kiss that man until her lips fell off.

Maybe Dennis was right today when he said she shouldn't have let him stay. He didn't like the way Brandon's eyes were always on her. He said it made him uncomfortable. She wondered what her brother would say if he saw the way she just looked at him, or could hear her thoughts. She cringed with embarrassment as she recalled the twinkle in Brandon's eyes while he feigned an apology for the encounter. Could he read her thoughts?

She listened to the stairs creek when Dennis came upstairs and knocked on Brandon's door. She heard her brother offer to take her guest to town and Brandon's request for assistance with his gelding. When Dennis popped his head in her room to fill her in on their plans she feigned a migraine and asked him to say her good-byes to Brandon and to assure him his gelding was welcome if he wanted to leave him behind for a little longer. She just couldn't face him.

Ten minutes later, she sat with her elbows on the window sill and her chin cradled in the palm of her hands while she watched Dennis and Brandon struggling to load the enormous gelding into the horse trailer. With calculated teamwork they coaxed the feisty gelding up the trailer ramp and were off down the drive. Tara felt both relief and disappointment as she stared out the window long after the SUV and trailer disappeared. She couldn't get the image of Brandon's nakedness out of her mind.

NINE

Dominic's broad smile greeted Tara when she pulled the door open. Her childlike look of delighted surprise tugged at him in earnest. It took all his reserve to refrain from taking her in his arms and holding her close. Firelight curls hung in disarray around her face and her flushed cheeks accentuated the blue in her oval eyes. They were so rich and deep he could see his reflection in them.

She was acutely aware of her appearance. Not anticipating company, she dedicated her day to fixing the crack in the wall in the bathroom that Brandon had reported. It wasn't going as well as she'd hoped. She was actually standing back debating about the prospect of calling in a professional when she heard Dominic's knock on the door. Dennis had suggested it several times and this was a time where she was sorry she hadn't listened.

"Did I interrupt something?" he questioned after surveying her boldly.

"I'm making the major decision of whether or not to call in the troops for this project or still try to go it alone," she explained. "You're a pleasant surprise and a reason to stop."

"I thought I'd pop over and make sure everyone was fine," he explained. "Your friend, the one with the injury to the head, is he well?"

Although his voice had a note of concern, the twinkle in his eye gave Tara reason to wonder.

"I guess so. I hardly know the man," she said flippantly.

For some unexplainable reason, discussing Brandon with Dominic left Tara feeling agitated. She felt an unspoken form of competition between the two. It was more than just for her attentions. It went deeper. Yet she was certain they had never met before the accident. In fact, Brandon couldn't even remember him once he regained consciousness. He'd vocalized gratitude for Dominic's help that day but he never expressed a desire to meet him and thank him personally.

"The way you cradled his head on the way to the hospital gave me the impression you were close," said.

His eyes bore into her as he awaited her response.

"I'm a compassionate woman," she said hesitantly, "and I wasn't cradling him. Not really."

Tara was extremely uncomfortable with the direction their conversation was going. The last thing she wanted was for Dominic to discover how she reacted to the mere mention of Brandon.

"Oh the female heart," he chuckled. "I guess perhaps I was misinterpreting the natural female tendency to nurture for more."

"Perhaps you were," she smiled.

The two stood in silence for a bit longer before he shifted his weight and admired the fields.

"It's really pretty and peaceful out here," he said thoughtfully. "How are the winters?"

"I'm assuming they're cold. I rarely visited my grandmother in the winters. My brother and I have done a lot of work on the house so we'll see what happens this year. I'm shooting for cozy," she replied.

"Ah, yes, cozy" he craned his neck to look past her. "You're on the right path from what I can see."

She stepped back from the doorway, suddenly aware of her rudeness.

"I'm sorry, I'm being rude. It's just that I wasn't expecting any company," she absent-mindedly smoothed her hair, "so you took me by surprise. You're welcome to come in."

She stood back to let him enter. He gave a quick nod of his head and moved past her, stopping at the doorway to the sitting room and staring at the fireplace. She joined him and followed his gaze to the gilded framed portrait over the mantelpiece. An old cracked portrait of a handsome elderly woman that bore stark contrast to its new framing hung precariously over it.

"That's my great grandmother. I found it in the attic and felt an odd attachment to her," Tara muttered as waived her hand indicating for him to take a seat.

Dominic's eyebrows raised in concentration while he poured over the portrait inch by inch, as if to absorb the woman into memory.

"She was quite a looker," he said.

Tara chuckled, "Would you like a cocktail or coffee or tea?"

"You drink? How metropolitan," he said with surprise and then caught himself. Insulting her wasn't his intention. It was just that he knew she'd only just turned eighteen and the offer of alcohol surprised him. "I'm sorry. What I meant is that I'm not much of a drinker in the afternoons, but for some reason it feels right. What do you have?" His mood lightened as he positioned himself on the sofa. The coziness of the decor and the bright sun gleaming through the new windows she installed almost as soon as she moved in gave a welcoming effect. "I like the way you're updating the place without stripping it of its historic charm."

"Brandy?" she asked as she smiled warmly.

"Brandy would be great," he replied. "Will you join me?"

"It's just what I need. It's been a hectic few weeks," she smiled as she handed him a snifter and lifted hers in a gesture of toasting.

They sipped in silence, listening to the sounds of nature outside. The thick leaves on the trees blanketed the hillside in rich shades of yellow and green that swayed in the strong wind that picked up outside. The heavy branches of the ancient oak tree scraped lightly across the roof as it unburdened itself, little by little, lending to the sensation of coziness in the room.

"Look at that wind pick up," Tara said with obvious concern.

"Yes," Dominic said. He smiled and stretched lazily, "Winter is on the horizon; a time of death for so much in nature. Death can be beautiful. Don't you think?"

"I suppose," she replied, "but I wasn't thinking of the beauty. My mind was focused on the fact that I have a huge mess upstairs in the one end of the house and I'm at a loss as of how to correct. The carpenters I've found are so busy I'm afraid I won't get it fixed before my aunt arrives for her visit. I'd hate to have her see it; not to mention the outside is actually coming inside and the cold weather will be here before we know it."

"I have a small amount of knowledge in home repairs," he offered. "I can't guarantee anything, but maybe I can provide some assistance. Can I take a look?" He stood up and placed his snifter gently on the coffee table and walked toward the servant's stairs without waiting for Tara. "Is it this way?" he asked over his shoulder.

Tara stared at the man in startled disbelief only briefly before scurrying to catch up. She stopped at the top of the narrow stairwell; surprised and relieved to see Dominic removing his jacket and rolling up his sleeves. Saying nothing to her, he immediately set to task correcting some of her poor patching.

Dominic's hands moved diligently, as if with a mind of their own, and three hours later he'd smoothed down the last of the plaster.

"This will have to be tackled from the outside as well you know," he said. "I'll leave you a list of supplies I'll need and I'll stop back in a few days to do the job. We need to wait for a less windy time. I don't know how to fly."

He chuckled at his own joke as he cleaned up the work space.

Tara nodded her head gratefully while helping clean up.

"I can't thank you enough. You're my knight in shining armor," she almost cooed. Realizing the way she sounded, she immediately shifted the mood, "I must pay you. Come downstairs. Is a check alright? I don't have much cash on me."

Her body lightly brushed against his as she scurried past him toward the stairs and a jolt of energy brought her senses alive. She sucked in air, excused herself and turned away; certain the heated color in her face would be noticed. What was wrong with her lately? First she couldn't control her reactions around Brandon and now Dominic. She'd been around plenty of handsome, charismatic men in her lifetime. Is this what happened to people living in seclusion?

He smiled knowingly as he placed his hand above her elbow. She stopped, still looking away. He pulled her chin gently until she faced him and held her gaze while he softly placed his lips on hers. She fell against him, wrapping her slender arms around his neck as she kissed him back with unplanned passion. His complete abandonment was infectious and it wasn't long before she found herself reciprocating. He embraced her passionately while he guided her to the same guest room Brandon had occupied. His strong hands held her close. She moaned as his sensuous kisses covered her face and throat.

The two were so lost in the magic of the moment they didn't hear Maggie open the front door and call out for Tara. Having searched the downstairs, she was just starting up the servants steps when her ears strained to identify the sounds. It was undeniably two people kissing and moaning. Tempted by curiosity, she ascended the stairs with surprising ease. Moving swiftly, she placed herself outside the door of the guest room and cleared her throat.

"I don't mean to interrupt," she barked. "I didn't realize you had...err...company."

Tara shoved Dominic from her in a panicked frenzy and fussed with her face and hair in an attempt to set herself aright and quickly flew off the bed. Dominic wasn't as accepting of the intrusion and made his feeling clear with a look that could kill.

"I'll go check on Sugar," Maggie said as she shot a dangerous look right back at him.

I'm coming," Tara called after her as she hurried to realign her clothes.

"I'll be on my way then," Dominic said.

"I have to pay you," she stammered.

"You just did," he chuckled seductively.

She wasn't sure she could get any more flushed than she felt at that moment,

"You'll be back in a few days?" she asked.

"I'll call you later with the list of things I'll need," he said with a smile.

****

Since that very first afternoon of what Tara reflected upon as sensual spontaneity, Dominic made it a point to drop by about the same time every day. Maggie, who was consistent with her visits as well, grew quiet and distant while she observed the relationship between the two unfolding. She grew suspicious when she noticed Tara acted dependent on his visits and pointed this out Tara; who responded with a gentle laugh and brushed her concerns away as over protectiveness. Maggie did her best to be civil and polite to Dominic, but the growing strain between them was apparent.

The days turned into weeks as the couple bonded. It didn't come as much of a surprise to Maggie when Tara announced she was in love with Dominic and was ready to take their relationship to the next level. She listened intently to Tara's musing about how wonderful Dominic was and how helpful he'd been with repairing her home.

Tara was so engrossed in the topic of Dominic and his wonderful attributes that she failed to notice the frown on Maggie's face or determination in her walk when she quickly excused herself and made her way across the meadow toward her own home.

Maggie was so busy fussing about Dominic and her concerns about Tara she was home before she knew it. She immediately set about her kitchen pulling out herbs and spices and mixing them in a large wooden bowl. When they were blended to her satisfaction, she slowly ladled it into the hot liquid she'd already prepared and had simmering on the stove in a thick cast iron cauldron. A vaporous, aromatic cloud arose and filled the room.

She stood motionless and stared into the cloud while an image formed in it. Then a whole scene formed clear and distinct. She saw Dominic standing amongst wolves, mountain lions, snakes, rats and bats. His face was distorted with rage and evil. Mice and rats scurried all around him. Maggie jumped back from the vision as it suddenly shifted and Brandon Wagner rode in the darkness on his large black gelding. She could feel his power as he grew larger and his body glowed with brilliant light.

"I was wrong! I had the wrong man!" Maggie wailed.

Having sensed evil around Tara, Maggie drugged Brandon and took blood to test for demonic traces but found nothing abnormal about him. Shortly after his visit, the energy around Tara mellowed so she felt the evil was gone, but it wasn't. It was masked from her by the true demon; Dominic.

She threw her hands to her head. The impact of her discovery connected her to evil energy that was so powerful she felt it would burst. She fell to the floor and lay totally devoid of strength for several hours before she was able to move.

****

As hard as Maggie tried, she couldn't get Dominic's evil image out of her mind. She sat on her porch that evening and sipped a cup of tea while she pondered what course of action to take next. She now knew what Dominic was and what she had to do. It was just a question of how to do it.

Tara insisted she loved him. If she didn't do something soon Tara would be lost. His kisses were slowly sucking the natural pure life force from the lass like a vampire and replacing it with his own evil pollution. Maggie could see it even if Tara couldn't.

She finished her tea and rose out of the rocker. The sun rested on the edge of the hilltop, casting shadows on its lush shades of browns, yellows and greens. As she peered out over the fields toward the edge of the woods, her gaze settled on a small form. She ran inside and grabbed her binoculars to get a better look. As she stood at the edge of the porch and raised them up in the direction of the form her suspicions where confirmed. It was another one of those demon wolves she killed at Tara's house the night Brandon visited. She now understood what they were and why they'd come. She calmly lowered her binoculars and went back into the house to retrieve her rifle. When she returned outside, the number of beasts had increased.

"So ya found me," she grumbled. "Well, if a fight's what ya want, a fight's what you'll get."

She put her rifle down and grabbed a broom to sweep the porch as if not to notice the evil creatures as they inched closer and closer toward her. Angus found his way onto the porch next to Maggie and snarled threateningly. She urged him to stay quiet while monitoring the creatures until they were close enough to see clearly without the binoculars. She counted six in all, but sensed there were more. Reaching for the box of ammunition she set on the small table she loaded her rifle and prepared a spare clip which she slid into her pocket.

With the accuracy and ease of someone familiar with weapons, she shot the beasts. One by one they burst into oblivion. They moved with surprising speed, leaving barely enough time to exchange the empty clip with the full one before the last three reached the porch. Angus attacked the leader with fervor.

Maggie destroyed the other two and turned to the battling duo. Angus's blood was everywhere as the beast got the better of him. Maggie's heart twisted when she realized her longtime friend was close to death. She took a chance and shot as their entwined bodies rolled past her. Angus yowled as the bullet caught him in the hip. She'd missed her mark, but it was enough to get the attention of the beast away from Angus and back to her.

She barely had time to blink before the creature raced toward her. His hot fowl breath assaulted her senses as his weight took them both to the floor. She fought, struggling to keep his long fangs from reaching their mark. The beast was bowled to the side as Angus was again on the attack. With lightning speed, Maggie was back on her feet; this time determined not to miss. The demon beast exploded and Angus fell to the floor, no longer able to find the strength to move.

Maggie kicked aside bits and pieces of rubbery flesh as she made her way to her beloved pet and companion. His labored breathing accentuated the blood that flowed out of his neck and hip. She ran into the house and returned with an oversized bath towel. Slowly, she rolled him onto the absorbent terry and pulled his bulk into the kitchen in front of the sink. She filled a bowl with clean water and went about the task of cleaning her faithful dog's wounds. It was the better part of an hour before she was confident that he was stable enough to lift onto the harvest table nearby. His eyes belied his condition as she gently laid him on the well-used wooden surface.

She moved with intent on completing her task as quickly as possible, Angus's life depended on it.

It was almost midnight before the bullet was removed and Angus lay, bandaged and comfortable on the mattress she'd pulled off her bed and dragged to the corner of her bedroom. She snuggled up next to him and wrapped her arms around him lovingly.

"We go together when we go old boy. Do ya hear me?"

she choked out. "You're not to leave me here alone. We go together when we go."

Angus licked her feebly as if to acknowledge the deal and the two dropped off into a deep, undisturbed sleep.

The following morning, Angus nudged Maggie to wake up. He'd managed to get out of bed and limp toward the door. She opened her eyes in surprise and immediately leapt up to open the door. Angus hobbled off the porch and went to his favorite tree to relieve himself. She rushed into the bathroom to do the same.

She and Angus ate a hearty breakfast of eggs and steak. When he'd cleaned his bowl and she her plate, she tidied up the kitchen and braced herself for what had to be done next. With the fear and worry of Angus subdued she could concentrate on getting Tara away from that evil demon man.

Maggie pulled out her books and leafed through the pages. After looking through three books with no results she closed her eyes in frustration.

"Where are ya now when I need your advice? What to do for Tara? I need your help," she moaned as she stared at the closed book.

The book flew open and the pages fanned until they settled on one. The old woman smiled as she read the words that were almost jumping off the page. It wasn't long before she was empowered with the right spell and got up to collect the items needed.

The day turned into evening before she eased her weary body into her favorite wooden rocker on the porch. Angus hobbled up to place his head in her lap and she stroked him affectionately.

"'Twas a long day me friend," she said lovingly, "but we've done it. Now, let's see what happens from here."

The stress, trauma and exertion of the last few days left her feeling old and tired. She longed for her lost youth. As she continued to rock on the porch she slowly drifted into a trance like state and saw herself in another time.

Her cottage was the same but her clothing was from a century earlier and her rocker was made of slender rustic logs instead of the smooth hardwood she enjoyed. Off in the distance Tara was dressed in similar fashion as she picked her way through the fields on her mare with her head tilted back to allow the sun past the broad rim of her bonnet. It was a contented scene.

Maggie was startled back to reality by Angus's snarls. She struggled to focus on the darkness that surrounded her. A loud clanging came from the direction of the shed out back. She stroked her dog to calm his wounded body down and then scurried inside for her rifle and a large flashlight before heading to the back door to take a closer look. She was extra alert after the events of the night before as she peered into the darkness; wishing old age had not taken such a hold on her eyesight.

When a tall staggering form flung itself from behind the shed she called for him to stop or she would shoot, but he ignored her warning and kept staggering forward. She set her flashlight on the porch in a manner that would aid with her visibility and raised her rifle to shoot and then hesitated. It was clear that the form was a man, not a demon, and there was something familiar about him. As recognition set in, she leaned her rifle against the porch post and rushed to help him.

"Dennis me boy, what are ya doing here? What happened to ya?" she rambled as she reached Dennis just in time to break his fall.

She laid him on the cool grass and stretched his limp form to make him as comfortable as possible. Her hands were sticky from the warm blood oozing from his body. Regretting the need to abandon him for even the briefest moment, she rushed back into the porch to retrieve her flashlight and surveyed the shadows for whatever attacked him while returning. The blood flowed from the gaping hole in his neck at a steady rate. If she didn't stop the bleeding soon, it would be too late.

Abandoning him one more time she rushed to the

kitchen and pulled down an old tin container from the corner shelf. It was coated with dust from lack of use. Scowling, she opened the lid and sniffed for freshness. She wanted the bleeding stopped before she assisted him in taking one more step and this powder, one of her mother's recipes, was the quickest way to do it. Thank goodness it was still usable.

Grabbing a towel from the sink, she returned to Dennis to do what she could to be able to move him. The bleeding stopped on contact with the powdery herb. Dennis wailed and writhed from the burning sensation it created but she never faltered. Within moments she transformed the towel into a bandage and helped him up onto his feet and into the house.

As they entered the bedroom, she realized her mattress was still on the floor in the corner and all that was left was the box springs.

"'Twill have to do for now," she muttered as she eased Dennis down. "Aye, this man's full of holes."

She gasped when blood from a lesser wound soiled the fabric. She scrambled for more of the herb powder and cloths. Maggie finally got his bleeding stopped and the wounds cleaned. She stood back and shook her head at the blood-soaked box spring. There was no saving it.

Angus came up beside her and nudged her gently. She realized that neither of them had eaten since breakfast. She stroked his head and made her way to the kitchen. There was a little left-over stew in the refrigerator that would do just fine. The old woman was simply too tired to bother to heat it up so she divvied it between the two of them and ate it cold. When their bellies where content, the old woman and her dog made their way to the mattress on the floor and fell into a deep slumber.

TEN

Tara paced back and forth the full length of her porch while wringing her hands. Dennis' argument with Dominic was so severe. She hadn't expected such a violent reaction from her brother when she told him she loved Dominic and he asked her to marry him. She didn't understand. Dennis' desire for her happiness over the years was a sincere desire, so why would he be so against it?

She wrestled with her thoughts. His concern that she didn't know much about Dominic had a ring of truth to it. She'd never even been to his home. In fact, she really hadn't been anywhere with him except her home and that one drive to the hospital when Brandon was injured, but it didn't matter. She loved him and she just knew they were meant to be together. Not everyone courted the same way. Hadn't he heard of love at first sight? His paranoia was unfounded. He had to get used to it. He had to.

Maggie's figure making her way up the drive caught her attention and she raced down the stairs to greet her. Maggie listened intently, without interruption, as Tara breathlessly told of the events the night before.

"It was just awful Maggie," Tara wheezed the words as she struggled to catch her breath. "The two were circling each other. Literally circling each other! I couldn't believe it. Dennis was so set on Dominic leaving and never coming back. And Dominic... Oh Maggie, he looked so mean. I've never seen him look so angry and mean before. His beautiful brown eyes were dark and sinister looking. It scared me a little! He stormed out of the house without a glance in my direction! I argued with

Dennis that he should be happy for me. I love Dominic. I feel like we're bonded in a way. Can you understand? Can you?"

"Yes lass. I understand more than ya realize," Maggie clicked out as she moved past Tara to sit on the porch chair she favored whenever she visited. The early morning walk took the little bit of strength she had left. "Fetch me a cup of tea, will ya? I'm a bit feeble this morning."

Focusing on preparing tea helped Tara calm down. When she returned with the beverage, Maggie sipped it gratefully while watching Tara over the brim of the cup.

"He left here for a walk last night. He was so angry," Tara moaned. "He hasn't come back. That's not like him. I mean, he's left before when we've argued but he's always returned after a few hours. He likes to walk and think. It clears his mind."

"Are ya talking about Dennis or Dominic, lass?" Maggie asked quietly. She knew it was Dennis, but decided to keep his whereabouts to herself while she sized up the situation.

"Oh, sorry," Tara apologized. "Dennis. I'm talking about Dennis. He must be really angry not to come back all night. I wonder where he stayed. It was pretty chilly last night so he couldn't have camped out anywhere. His car is still here."

"Not to worry lass. He's fine wherever he is. Now, tell me about this Dominic fella. Why did he get so mad at Dennis? Didn't he expect to have some trouble with the family? He's pretty new and all," Maggie said as she set her cup down on the table and stretched her legs in front of her.

They talked for almost three hours while Maggie pumped Tara for as much information as she could get. Tara answered freely. By the time they finished Maggie had drawn a pretty clear picture of what had happened to Dennis while on his way through the woods. This Dominic was bad news. He had to be stopped. Maggie silently prayed that the spell she cast would be effective.

Morning turned into afternoon before Maggie rose to leave. She stopped half way down the porch steps to observe the large white taxi pulling up the drive. The electricity in the air from an oncoming storm energized the mare more than normal and she seized the opportunity to squeal her challenge to the vehicle for a race. Maggie smiled. She found that horse to be a genuine delight.

As the cab stopped in the circular part of the long drive, Tara stood on the porch with surprised curiosity as she watched Brandon Wagner climb out, pay the driver, and send the cab away. When he finally did acknowledge her, it was in a calm and matter-of-fact mannerism while he walked up to her slowly, tilting the cap on his head. Maggie decided to stick around a while longer and returned to her cup of tea and comfortable chair on the porch. She'd left the two of them on the opposite side of the wraparound porch but made certain she was able to hear enough of their muffled voices to understand what was happening.

"Hello there!" Brandon said with a smile that Tara found captivating.

"This is a surprise," Tara said. "What brings you here?"

Tara's confusion was genuine. She hadn't seen nor heard from Brandon since she encountered his naked body in the hallway. Although she still remembered the encounter vividly, he apparently didn't.

"Would you believe I was in the neighborhood?" he drawled sheepishly.

"You were pretty confident you would find me home and you'd be welcome," Tara drawled as she stepped aside to allow Brandon onto the porch. "You let the cab go right away."

She chuckled, finding humor in the situation.

"I'm psychic," he grinned as he strolled into the house without waiting for an invitation.

Maggie found them in the living room and quickly approached Brandon, extending her large rough hand for him to shake. The enthusiasm in her movements was exceeded by her greeting. Tara stood back, watching curiously. She'd never seen Maggie this excited about meeting up with anyone and she really didn't think she harbored any type of fondness for Brandon. She wondered about the sudden change. Her curiosity made her forget about the argument between Dennis and Dominic the night before and the fact that Dennis hadn't returned.

The trio talked and laughed about any topic that came to mind for over an hour. When Dominic arrived at his usual time, Tara jumped with a start. She'd completely forgotten about him. Normally she spent her hours watching the clock with anticipation.

The surprised look on her face when he entered the house didn't go unnoticed by Dominic and he glowered at Brandon unappreciatively while motioning for Tara to follow him. She surprised both Brandon and Maggie when she excused herself and obeyed.

"Do you really think this is a good idea?" Tara asked as she reached the top landing of the stairwell. She was uncomfortable about leaving Maggie and Brandon like she did.

"What do you mean?" Dominic's voice was almost a growl as he urged her into the den. His movements very closely resembled pushing.

"We have guests. It doesn't seem right to leave them sitting downstairs. What will they think?" Tara said as she kissed Dominic on the cheek and made move to leave the room. "Let's go back downstairs before they get the wrong idea."

"What idea is that?" Dominic asked as he grabbed Tara's arm and prevented her from moving. "The idea that we are two people in love?"

He wrapped his arms around her, pinning her motionless.

"You could look at it that way," she giggled, "but you could also look at it as being rude."

Tara tried to free herself but Dominic only tightened his hold on her. She didn't like the feeling of being trapped like this and struggled even harder.

"Dominic, please," she whispered harshly.

"Please, what?" he asked as she brought his mouth to hers so forcefully her lips pained and she was sure they were bleeding.

Her body hardened in defiance of her lover's actions but instead of easing up, he kissed her more forcefully, almost cutting off her breathing.

Dominic wrestled with the urge to force Tara to do his bidding. Things weren't going well and time was running short. Between his argument with Dennis and the arrival of Brandon, the threat of Tara changing her mind about him loomed heavy. It didn't help that the old woman was down there getting cozy with Brandon. Did she think he didn't know what she was up to? He cursed himself for not finishing Brandon off that day in the clearing when he had the chance. If he hadn't been so worried about Tara catching him in the act he'd be free of his threat. Maybe if he hadn't offered to take that pest to the hospital... Well, what was done was done. He needed to worry about what to do instead of what he should have or could have done. He couldn't afford to have any more setbacks. The eve of the thinning of the veil was soon and it was vital that he find the key. The only reason he'd even offered to help her with the house repairs was to give him an opportunity to look for it. He needed to move in with her so he could look more thoroughly without suspicion. She was old enough to make up her own mind and he almost had her talked into it. He even offered marriage to appease her desire to remain untouched until she was wed. What more could he do? Something other than that bothersome brother of hers blocked it from happening. He suspected the old woman was linked to it somehow. She would have to be reckoned with as soon as possible.

He eased his grip on Tara and put his lips gently to her ear, "Just a moment my love. Give me just a moment and then we can go down, okay?"

She shuddered with delight as Dominic's lips gently

caressed her ear. She felt herself melting in his arms and forgetting about all else. She loved being in his arms. He had a way of making her forget the world outside.

Happy he accomplished his mission, Dominic gently released her and walked to the mini bar he'd suggested she set up for second floor convenience.

"Let's have one drink alone before we rejoin our guests, shall we?" he asked. "Call me selfish, but I hate to share you. I love you so much."

Like a giddy school girl, she readily agreed. They had only been gone from Maggie and Brandon a few minutes so an intimate drink with her fiancé wouldn't be a problem. They would still return in time for their guests to realize nothing else went on.

She scowled when she realized she referred to Maggie as a guest.

"It's a little chilly in here. We won't be here long enough to justify a fire, but can you pull the drapes closed? Those windows still leak," Dominic asked.

He wasn't in the least bit cold, but he needed some reason to occupy Tara's attention so she wouldn't see him reach in his pocket and pour the contents of a small vile into her glass of brandy. He knew she would have preferred wine but brandy camouflaged the taste better. To his delight, she fussed over the draperies in an effort to seal the windows as much as possible before rejoining him, providing him ample time to mix the potion thoroughly.

He placed a soft kiss on her lips while he slid the glass of brandy into her hand. He waited for her to protest and ask for wine and smiled when she didn't. Holding his up to indicate a toast and they gently clanked their glasses together before bringing the burning liquid to their lips. The potion was strong and it took only one or two sips of the brandy before Tara's head grew light and disorientation set in. Dominic grabbed the glass that still contained the drugged brandy and set it on a nearby table before gently guiding her toward the sofa.

He watched her with a satisfied grin. Time was too short to take any chances. He needed continual access to the house. It was a shame his magical skills were limited outside of Shadow Land. Things would have been finished by now if he had his full faculties about him. Since time was running out and he needed her to let him move in willingly he saw no other option than to take her innocence and impregnate her. With her family's old-fashioned ways, she and her brother were sure to insist on an immediate marriage. He scrutinized the room and smiled. He'd always coveted this house and finally, after centuries of waiting, it would soon be his. He thought about the rewards that awaited him, not just for locating the crystal, but finally enslaving the famous enchantress.

When Dominic first met up with Tara in the grove, he had to stifle the emotions that threatened to surface and ruin everything. He hadn't expected seeing her would heighten the flame of his desire for revenge and to force her to do his bidding for eternity.

"You'll soon be bound to me for eternity, my love," Dominic whispered as he slowly unbuttoned her camp shirt. "You lose. That pest you call brother loses and that old woman downstairs... well, let's just say things are going to change around here, shall we?"

****

Maggie watched Brandon pace the room.

"How long has this been going on?" he growled.

"Where did ya disappear to?" she asked. "The girl has a crush on ya. Ya could have easily stopped this."

"It couldn't be helped," he hissed. He regarded Maggie thoughtfully for a moment before asking, "Do you remember me?"

"Have ya lost your mind?" she gasped.

"We need to talk," he continued.

"That may be so, but not now. Something's going on up there that doesn't feel right," she spat as she burst from the chair and bounded up the stairs.

Brandon hesitated only a second before he was on her heels.

The den door was locked. Maggie called out for Tara to open it but was greeted by silence. She knew they were on the other side of the door and she also knew Tara didn't respond to her because she couldn't.

"How tough is your shoulder?" she asked as she motioned for Brandon to break down the door.

"We'll find out," he replied as he stepped back and put all his might into his charge.

The wood near the doorknob splintered enough for them to force the door opened. Brandon's chest heaved with indignation at the scene before him. Tara lay on the sofa with her clothes in disarray. She was clearly drugged.

"I'll kill you!" he bellowed as he charged Dominic.

Dominic barely had time to stand before Brandon's full on charge knocked him down.

The two men were a pretty even match in strength and fury. While they rolled, punched, and growled threats, Maggie rearranged Tara's clothes to preserve her modesty. She held her wrist and took her pulse. It was steady. When she pulled up a limp eyelid Tara's eye moved in response to the light. She had no sooner come to the conclusion that her young friend would regain consciousness soon when Tara stirred. She helped her come around by lightly tapping her cheeks and upper arms.

"What happened?" Tara slurred as she pulled herself up.

"He drugged ya," Maggie spat.

Tara gasped at the sight of Brandon and Dominic fighting.

"Stop! Stop it!" she screamed.

Her unexpected outburst stopped the men immediately. They untangled from each other and stood apart, each one coiled for action should the other want to begin again.

"What's happening?" Tara cried. "I feel so..."

"Drugged?" Brandon spat while looking accusingly at Dominic.

"You drugged me?" she asked in a hurtful tone to Dominic.

When he didn't make an effort to deny it, or even explain why, she demanded he leave her home.

Dominic glowered at Maggie and Brandon before backing out of the room. The air was thick with his hate and evilness. Maggie waved her hand as if to push it away.

"We'll be waiting downstairs," Maggie said to Tara as she signaled Brandon to follow her with her head. "Take your time coming down."

****

Maggie was already sipping on her brandy by the time Brandon joined her. She knew he hadn't immediately followed her and she also knew he, like Tara, needed time to process what just happened.

"I thought you were part of it," she said as Brandon entered the room. "Especially after that night when ya was visiting and the woods was filled with the wolf beasts, but when I studied your blood sample it showed me nothing. I got confused."

Brandon grabbed his arm and scowled.

"How did you get my blood?" he asked, although he suspected he already knew.

"I slipped a sedative in your drink and I took it," she replied matter-of-factly.

Although he was angered by her actions, he said nothing. He'd had enough fighting for the day.

"Just before she met ya, she read from the book and brought forth the dark side. It ripped up the place, but her spirits helped hold it back. Thanks for that." she heaved a sigh. "It must have got loose anyway. It's mighty strong, stronger than I thought in the beginning and it wants her. Not only does it want her, it wants this place. He tried to move in with her. He was pushing for marriage. Her brother would have none of it and they had a wicked fight. Dennis is at my place now. A demon creature attacked him. I think those creatures are connected to the demon man we just saved Tara from."

Brandon's eyes grew large as he listened. Recognition set in and he finally knew the truth of the matter. Although Maggie was still in the dark, she slowly came to know it too. He sat on the edge of his chair while the old woman continued.

"I think Dominic is the leader," Maggie continued. "He's damn good ya know. He had me looking in your direction for the bad he did. His actions were very odd; like how he never took her out of the house. The man drives a Mercedes and wears fine clothes. I find it hard to believe he can't afford to take the lass out to dinner or a movie once in a while. Instead, he visits for a few hours each afternoon at the same time; spending part of it kissing and the other part repairing the house. You can imagine the chaos that went on when she announced her intention to marry him."

"She agreed to marry him?" Brandon shifted uncomfortably in his chair.

"'Twas hard to watch her change like that," Maggie said as she shook her head. "I finally pulled out one of me ma's books and did what I had to do to help the situation."

"What was that?" Brandon asked, still not clear on what she was saying.

"I summoned ya. Or should I say that I summoned the one person that could help, not knowing who it would be," Maggie said as she got up to pour more bandy into her glass.

"I don't follow," Brandon mused.

"Sit back Lad. It'll all make sense to ya in a minute," she soothed.

"I really hope so ma'am," Brandon breathed out the words as he fell back into the chair to hear Maggie's story. His talk with her could wait.

"Ma'am?" she raised her eyebrows and wrinkled her

brows like she was straining to remember. He thought she remembered until she said, "Never mind." She waived her hand in dismissal and continued. "Why did ya come here?"

Her demanding tone took Brandon by surprise.

"I'm not really sure," he answered honestly. "I planned on coming in a few days to visit but I woke up and decided to come today."

"Ya came because ya were summoned by the spirits to help her. You're connected somehow on a soul level. Have ya any understanding of what I'm saying?" she asked.

"Yes I do," he smiled.

She had no idea how close to the truth her statement was, but he guessed she would remember soon enough.

"I know ya do," Maggie said with confidence. "I know it. Deep inside ya lies the knowledge. Ya both have it. She's a flower waiting to bloom and you're the gardener tending her soil."

Maggie paused a moment as if to contemplate what she said. She walked over to pour herself more brandy. It was unlike her to drink so heavily but these last few days were unlike any she'd experienced before. She would have to stop after this one though. She just wanted to settle herself down, not get drunk.

"Little by little, day after day, that demon was slowly sucking Tara's will from her body until she would eventually be like a zombie doing his bidding," Maggie explained. "Don't get me wrong. She'd be alive, but she'd have no will of her own and would answer only to his desires and wishes. I could see it happening. You witnessed it yourself." She heaved a sigh, "Tara doesn't know about Dennis yet. I didn't want her to tell that demon fella his whereabouts so he could finish him off." Maggie tossed down the remainder of her drink and went back to sit in the chair she loved so much. She eased into it slowly, as if she'd suddenly aged a lifetime, "Anyway, he's got his hands full with you here. He'll want to be rid of you so Dennis is safe for now." She leaned forward and peered into his steel gray eyes.

"Don't ask me how I know. I just do. You're the one to end it all. Just follow your gut like ya did when ya came here."

Brandon decided this was prime time to have that conversation he'd wanted to have but Maggie cut him off and claimed she drank too much brandy and needed to lie down. She knew she should to go back to her place to check on Dennis, but she also felt she was needed there. It was a difficult decision. She called on her guides to watch over the young man and her beloved dog, and moved to the sofa to lie down. Not certain what the night would bring, she decided to get some rest and let the brandy wear off. She might need her faculties about her later on.

Brandon went to the kitchen and made himself a snack while he pondered over what to do next. Things were getting very complicated and time was running out. His allotted time there was almost up. He'd have to return soon. It was just his luck that neither Maggie nor Tara had their memories.

****

Rather than join Maggie and Brandon, Tara went to her room and slept long and hard. When she awoke, she lay cuddled under the covers and peeked through the gap in the draperies. It was early evening. Quickly looking over at the clock on the dresser, she was shocked to see it was after seven. She hadn't planned on sleeping that long.

She leapt out of bed too quickly. The blood rushing from her head forced her to hold the headboard until she could regain her composure. She felt exhausted as she made her way into the bathroom. Pieces of the events of the day came back to her. Uncertain if Maggie was still in the house, she hit the intercom button for the downstairs speaker and called out for her. After a few minutes with no response, she decided Maggie was gone. If Brandon was still there he either didn't hear the intercom or know how to use it. Either way, she felt a strong need to soak in a hot bath and decided to do just that before going down stairs to check things out.

She filled the tub with hot bubbles while sporadic, dream-like memories of the day's events floated through her mind. Finding a soothing CD, she placed it in the player and lit a scented candle. Easing herself deep beneath the bubbles, she burrowed into the warm liquid to soothe her muscles and hopefully wash away the fogginess from her brain. Although she was still unclear as to what she dreamt verses what had actually happened, she wasn't terribly bothered by it. She felt a strange sense of peace and contentment. It was a different kind of peace than the cozy one she was used to. It was a deep, peace. Something she could hardly explain to herself, let alone anyone else.

The music from the CD seemed to drift off into the distance as a large glowing ball appeared before her. She wasn't bothered by Liam's graceful entrance and remained calm and still as he stepped out of the glowing ball in a semitransparent state that radiated light. She said nothing as she watched his glowing figure move gracefully about the room until he positioned himself where she could see him without straining her neck. After a few moments of silence, he stepped so close she could reach out and touch him, but she didn't.

"Greetings. I come to speak to you this evening of the day's events," he said gently. She was suddenly alert. She kept her torso immersed in the bubbles and her ears eager to listen as Liam continued, "We have been watching with interest during the recent events in your life. Your associations have been less than perfect. Although this is a very good lesson in judgment for you, we fear the consequences may be dear. For this reason, we wish to extend our assistance to you as much as we are allowed. You have near you very dear souls who, together with you, will be able to stop the evil unleashed. We are in hopes this can be done without the need of our assistance but if not, you are to simply call. You must remember that we cannot interfere unless you ask. Call my name three times and help will be available. You are loved." Upon completion of his statement, Liam immediately returned to the glowing ball and was gone.

Tara lay still in the tepid bath water long after Liam disappeared into nothingness. She had so many questions that needed answers, yet she wasn't given the chance to ask even one. Who are the dear souls to help her? Is it Maggie? Dennis? What association is less than perfect? Dominic? Brandon?

Her skin was shriveled by the time she climbed out of the water. Rather than feeling relaxed and enlightened by Liam's visit, she was now tense and confused. She wrapped herself in a soft robe and started downstairs. Brandon and Maggie were sitting at the kitchen table in cozy conversation. They stopped when they saw her.

"There ya are," Maggie smiled, relieved to see Tara up and around.

Tara stood before Brandon with her hands on her hips, "Are you going to tell me what that was all about up there?"

"I don't follow," he said with surprise.

"Ya have no memory?" Maggie asked with surprise.

"I have eyes and a den that's been trashed by this hoo-ha and I'd like to know why," Tara spat. "Where's Dominic?"

"She doesn't remember," Brandon said incredulously and rose to leave. "I should go."

Maggie held up her hand in a gesture to signal him to stop where he was.

"Stay where ya are," she barked. "No one is going anywhere. Not just yet, anyway." She looked directly at Tara. "I want ya to sit there and listen to me for a bit while I try to explain what's been going on here. It's a bit hard to understand, so I'll take me time."

Tara reluctantly agreed and took the chair between Brandon and her dear friend.

Maggie spoke of times of old with demons and witches and sorcerers; times in her country when people believed in the undead and of possession.

Brandon listened with interest. Was Maggie saying

what he hoped? Did she remember after all?

Tara listened intently with not so much as a sound until Maggie reached the topic of Dominic. When she worked her way up to declaring Dominic a demon in disguise, Tara sucked in a breath of shock.

She rejected the notion vehemently.

"How can you say that?" she protested. "How? You know I'm in love with him. I couldn't fall in love with a demon, Maggie. Why is everyone so against him? You're wrong. You're terribly, terribly, wrong about him. I just know it."

"Know this and know it well," Maggie said with conviction. "Dominic is a demon. What he's been doing to ya every afternoon is sucking the life from ya so you'll have no mind of your own. He panicked when he saw Brandon here and drugged ya. He was going to rape ya, figuring if he made a baby your old-fashioned ways would make your brother agree to marriage. Brandon broke the door down just in time."

"No," Tara persisted. You're wrong". You have to be."

Tara fled from the room, tears of frustrated rage gushed down her cheeks.

Maggie stood in silence. It was going to be harder than she thought to break the demon man's hold on her young friend. Her body felt the strain of the last few days and she suddenly remembered Dennis and her beloved dog.

"Come lad," she said. Her voice sounded a little gruffer than intended. "I need to go and check on Dennis and I don't like the idea of leaving ya behind."

"No", Brandon mumbled. "I'll go. I should go."

"Ya need to come with me," Maggie insisted as she pulled Brandon onto his feet with the strength of an angry bull. "Once I see to Dennis we can sit out on the porch and ya can tell me whatever it is you've wanted to tell me all day." As they started for the door she said, "In fact, why don't ya start your story now. It'll take my mind off the fact that it's dark and we have to walk through the woods with those demon wolves on the loose.

"Do you have a flashlight?" he asked.

Maggie went into the pantry and pulled two flashlights from the top shelf. She smiled at the fact that her young friend had such a stock pile of supplies in preparation for a harsh winter that might include electric blackouts. It wasn't such a farfetched notion. The area was known to have a blackout or two during the worst winter weather, but this girl had enough candles and flashlights to light a village block. Maggie couldn't have been more grateful. She handed a flashlight to Brandon and they headed across the fields toward her home.

Even though going through the woods was the shortest route, they still had to walk a few miles to get to Maggie's cottage with half of it through thick woods. While they kept their eyes out for demon wolves, Brandon asked Maggie one more time if she remembered him. He debated about how much to tell her when she expressed her confusion over his question. Should he start in the beginning, middle or tell her just enough to jog her memory? He decided to start in the beginning.

The path was narrow in places and required they walk single file. Brandon walked behind Maggie, which prevented him from seeing her face as he spoke. Since she listened in silence he had no idea what she thought of his story. Would her memories come back? If not, was she at least open minded enough to believe in the probability of what he was telling her? She believed in magic. He'd seen her work it. Surely she wouldn't reject his story. He wished she could see her face.

Brandon talked for the majority of their three-mile walk. Just ahead was the clearing that led to her little cottage. They were also nearing the section where the demon wolfs came out the night before. She wanted to comment on what he had to say but she needed her fullest attention to scope for them.

He waited in silence for her to say something.

"Aren't you going to say anything?" he asked.

"Hush," she hissed as she shone the light into the trees.

"What is it?" he whispered into her ear from behind.

"Look," she whispered back as she wiggled the beam of the flashlight to indicate he look in that direction. "Do you see the eyes?"

He did. They were evil red, unnatural looking eyes that could only belong to Satan's pets. They were here. The question was, how many?

She moved the flashlight's beam in the direction of her cottage. She was glad Tara talked her into putting her porch light on a timer. It made it easy to see her house.

"Can we make it?" he asked with concern.

"I can run like the wind when I have to," she said flatly.

"How fast can they run is the question," he said.

"We're about to find out," she said as she burst into the fastest run she could manage across the recently cropped field.

Brandon reached down and removed his two-shot pocket pistol from its holder beneath his pant leg. He'd have to be close to a beast to be able to hit him with it but it was better than nothing. The time he took to grab his pistol was only seconds but it was long enough to put him a fair distance behind Maggie. She wasn't joking when she said she could run like the wind. The woman was amazing. Running across a rutted field in the dark with only a bobbing beam of light to illuminate the way proved taxing for Brandon. Maggie, on the other hand, knew her way so well she reminded him of a gazelle fleeing a predator. She didn't miss a beat. They were only yards from her front porch when a demon wolf came out of the darkness and knocked Maggie off her feet. He could see another rushing in and estimated it would reach them in a matter of seconds. His hand worked before his brain could even give it instructions and he shot the beast attacking Maggie before it could do anything more than assault her with its abominable breath. He turned just in time to kill the second beast as it soared in mid-air toward them.

"You're full of surprises," Maggie said as she picked

bloody shards of demon-wolf off her body.

"It's all I had," Brandon said as he helped her to her feet.

"Let's get inside," she replied before rushing to the porch and throwing open her front door. "Hurry," she called to him as he bounded onto the porch. "We got lucky. They travel in packs."

ELEVEN

Tara stretched her body across her bed as she stared at the antique lace canopy above. Frustration mixed with panic filled every fiber of her being. Was Maggie telling the truth? Why couldn't she remember being drugged by Dominic? What made Maggie think he was a demon?

She paced around the room, unsure of what to do next. She had to see Dominic. She needed to talk to him and straighten things out. If he'd just sit down with Maggie and let her get to know him, then Maggie would be able to see what a wonderful man he really was. Yes, that was it. She would go to Dominic and have him straighten things out with Maggie. She threw on a pair of jeans and a sweater, ran a comb through her hair, and headed downstairs.

As she closed the door behind her, the cool night air filled her lungs. Brilliant stars surrounded the full moon, lighting up the night for ample visibility. She walked past the den and peered in the window. There was no sign of Maggie and Brandon. She decided they must have remained in the kitchen after she ran out.

Happy to have gotten out without being noticed, she headed for the paddock. Her mare stood majestically while watching her approach. She stroked Sugar's mane and nuzzled her neck as she relived Maggie's words, 'Dominic's a demon. He's slowly sucking the life force from ya.'

Maggie's claim felt very real. Her eyes widened and her heart picked up pace as she absorbed the impact of this revelation. Dominic truly was a mystery and she really didn't know anything about him except that he was incredibly handsome, a fabulous kisser, and a fairly good repair man. They talked a little during his visits, but mainly about her house. To top it off, she couldn't go to see him because she didn't have a clue where he lived. The absurdity of it all was overwhelming. How could she have been so blind and foolish? This wasn't like her at all. She needed more answers. She needed help in understanding everything that happened since Dominic arrived at her house that afternoon. She needed Maggie.

Tara raced back to the house. She was finally ready to listen to what the old woman had to say. She would sit down quietly and give her full attention. She still couldn't perceive Dominic as a demon but she was certain he was up to something. Visions of his visits started rushing to her. What was his fascination with her house? He was overly attached to it, considering the short time they'd known each other. She questioned which meant more to him, the house or her. She should hear Maggie out. The old woman was dear to her and she trusted her completely. There must be a reason she thought him a demon; a bigger reason than the fact that she didn't like how cheap he was.

She entered the house and called for Maggie but all was silent. She checked the patio, knowing Maggie enjoyed sipping brandy in the moonlight but there was no sign of her, or Brandon for that matter. It was obvious Maggie left and since she hadn't noticed any vehicles coming up the drive to take Brandon away, she concluded he left with her. Maggie was such a private person. Why would she take Brandon to her home? Nothing made sense.

She made her way back out to the barn where Sugar stood waiting, as if knowing her mistress would be back shortly. Slipping the mare's bridle on with ease, Tara's impatience prompted her to forgo the saddle. Almost immediately after pulling herself onto the horse's back they were through the gate and moving swiftly across the field toward Maggie's cottage. The cool wind blew through her locks while they raced with the moonbeams. Shadows darted all around them, giving the night and eerie sensation.

As they approached the woods she slowed Sugar down to a steady walk. The crunching of the leaves and twigs rang out as they made their way along the narrow path through the thick array of trees. An owl hooted overhead, giving Tara quite a start. When she jumped, so did her mare. While she regained her seating Tara looked over her shoulder and discovered a pair of large red eyes staring at her from the distance through the darkness. Sugar must have noticed at the same time because she shuddered and picked up speed, tension clearly mounting in her body.

She regretted her decision to ride to Maggie's in the night; especially after the incident with the mysterious wolf creature. She considered returning home, but determined that she was past midway and it was shorter to Maggie's house so she pressed on.

Just as horse and rider neared the end of the woods a loud howl sounded behind them. Tara kicked Sugar into action as she sped across the field. The lights in the distance seemed tortuously far away as the howling grew louder. She heard hoofs pounding on the ground behind her and looked over her shoulder at the large dark figure racing toward her on equally dark horseback. Her heart competed with the pounding that was closing in on them.

Wild with panic, she kicked her heels into Sugar's sides and instantly regretted her decision not to use a saddle as she slid from side to side. Sugar pushed to her limit. The light in Maggie's window got bigger while the pounding of the horse's hooves behind her got fainter.

Tara felt indescribable relief when she reached the lawn and Maggie stepped out onto the porch. The old woman rushed forward just as Sugar slid to an abrupt stop and Tara tumbled onto the cool grass in a large ball. Maggie helped her up and, without hesitation pulled her into the house. To Tara's surprise, her friend immediately went back out for Sugar and coaxed her into the house as well.

"I have no barn," Maggie explained to the shocked people in her kitchen, "and the beasts are out there."

Sugar made her way over to the far side of the room where the furnishing was sparse. Angus approached the mare cautiously, but with the warmth of acceptance.

Tara surveyed the large open room that served as a kitchen, dining and sitting room. She was surprised to see Dennis and Brandon sitting next to each other with a game of chess between them. She forgot her curiosity about why Dennis was there when she saw her brother's bandaged body. He ignored his sister's reaction while he looked at her with concern in his eyes. He released the breath he'd absent-mindedly held when he was satisfied that she was fine.

"You're hurt!" Tara exclaimed as she rushed to Dennis' side. "How?" she asked as she touched his bandaged chest.

"Ouch! Be careful," he moaned. "I'm not sure what happened. I was walking through the grove and... I don't really know. Something attacked me." Dennis' face was pale and gaunt as he told his tale to the room. "It was this ugly, indescribable thing. It had the head of a wolf and the body of a huge cat. What would you even call something like that, a wolf-cat? I'm not sure."

Tara gasped as she recalled the beast at her house. This sounded like the same kind of creature. Maggie stepped across the room with interest. There was so much going on that she hadn't had the time to question Dennis about the source of his injuries.

"Go on lad", she prompted.

"I know it's hard to believe, but that's what it looked like," Dennis said. "I rolled on the ground with it and luckily there was this big bolder. We slammed against the boulder. This thing took most of the blow which must have knocked the wind out of it or something. Its grip weakened and I slipped free. I threw a rock at him as hard as I could and just ran. I don't know what happened after that. I ran blindly through the woods and the next thing I knew Maggie was taking care of me. That thing was damned ugly." He shuddered as he touched his bandage. "I hope it didn't have rabies or something."

"I didn't think of that," Maggie mused. "I doubt it, but we'd better get ya on something to prevent an infection. Some of those wounds are quite deep. Did it bite ya or claw ya? It was hard to tell."

"Both. It was full of claws and teeth. Its teeth felt like knives going in me and the stench! Its breath was putrid!" Dennis replied.

Brandon popped into the conversation, "It sounds like those creatures we killed tonight."

"You killed some?" Tara asked while looking at Maggie for the answer.

"We were attacked in the field outside," Maggie said and then smiled at Brandon. "Lucky he was carrying a little pee shooter in his pants."

"Strapped to my shin if you please," Brandon said with amusement.

"How can you find humor at a time like this?" Tara scolded.

"Never mind and sit," Maggie interrupted, "it's not important now. What is important is doing something to prevent any infections or diseases. It should've been done earlier, but I've had me hands full. Look at Angus over there, will ya? He had a similar encounter. 'Tis the demon's doing."

Maggie's chest heaved heavily as she thought of the work ahead of her. Her tired muscles longed for the comfort of her bed but it didn't look like that would happen any time soon.

"Get me book down from the shelf for me, please," she said to Tara, "the one with medicines written on it. I'll clear away the table. Let's fix up your brother and then we'll sit and discuss things."

Tara proved an eager student since she'd met the old woman and was familiar with Maggie's quirks and pattern of action. They worked in unison, with Tara second guessing Maggie's needs and requests prior to her asking. A smile of satisfaction spread across Maggie's handsome face as she watched her long hours of schooling and preparation with Tara come to bloom before her eyes. The lass moved about with the skill of the women of the old world.

Maggie focused on Tara's energy. There was something changing. She was a little startled and stepped back when a barely visible robed man stood behind Tara. A mellow, glowing emanated from him. Maggie knew she had the privilege of glimpsing Tara's spirit guide. Without warning, the figure of a woman stepped out of the robed man and encompassed Tara. The face of the spirit was the face of Maggie's great grandmother. Maggie rubbed her eyes in recognition as she stood silent.

Not sure what was wrong, and not feeling comfortable asking, Tara quietly waited for instructions from Maggie.

Brandon broke the mood when he cleared his throat. Maggie had closed the windows after bringing Sugar inside and he was hot and stuffy, not to mention the scent of horse filled the room.

Maggie recomposed herself and set to work. Within minutes she and Tara were standing in front of Dennis offering him spoonfuls of the herbal medicine. He coughed and gagged as they pushed the thick porridge-like mixture into his mouth; barely allowing him time to swallow. A long shutter ran through his body while he struggled to get down the last spoonful.

"Water," he gasped. "It's stuck!"

Brandon quickly drew a glass of water and handed it to Dennis. He was thankful it wasn't him being forced to down the disgusting muck. It smelled foul even from where he stood.

"You'll be fine," Maggie said in as soothing a tone as she could muster under the circumstances. "I know it's a bad taste but it'll kill anything trying to live in ya."

"It was like swallowing puke!" Dennis choked.

"That's disgusting," Tara whined and her stomach turned in reaction.

"Try some," Dennis said to his sister while he struggled to get the last of the mixture to go down his throat and into his stomach.

"I'll pass, thanks," she replied as she walked behind her brother and put her arms around him gently. She bent down and placed her cheek against his and spoke softly, "I trust Maggie. You needed that medicine no matter how bad it tastes. Those wounds should have been stitched. You're oozing blood!"

"Let me see lad," Maggie said as she gently pulled Tara back away from Dennis and move in closer. She lightly tugged a bandage far enough away so she could look behind it. "Ya need to stay as still as ya can for another day or so. Ya better go lie back down on the springs."

"Springs?" Brandon said, puzzled.

"Poor Maggie's overridden with patients," Dennis explained. "She and Angus have the mattress on the floor and I've got the box springs." Dennis smiled warmly at Maggie, "I have to say, dear lady, 'tis fit for a king. 'Tis the best sleep I've had in ages!"

Maggie chuckled at Dennis' attempt at an Irish brogue. She was glad to see he was able to project humor into the situation and ease the panic that could have easily mounted as the reality of the severity of their situation set in.

Renewed howling outside brought all chuckling to a halt. Brandon ran to the window while Dennis turned gray. Maggie ran to her shelf of books, returned the book-marked medicines and pulled down one labeled 'spells'. The spell book opened on its own when Tara pushed Maggie out of her way. The image of her great grandmother grew stronger as Maggie watched Tara run her finger down the page until she found the section she searched for. She tapped the page lightly and swung the book toward Maggie so she could read the page.

"Good!" Maggie exclaimed while she rushed to the corner cupboard in the pantry room and returned with a small box.

She gently removed the top to expose a neatly packed array of candles and incense. Disappearing back into the pantry room, she returned with an armful of candle holders. Selecting some black candles and a large white candle, Maggie secured them in the holders. Pushing furniture out of her way, she placed the large white candle on the floor in the center of the room and then the black ones in the four corners of the room before lighting a long twig and handing it to Tara.

"Say these words as you light each candle," she instructed as she took a loose piece of brittle, yellowed paper from the back of the book and handed it gently to Tara.

Tara immediately went to the black candles and lit them one by one. She repeated the words on the paper each time she lit a candle.

"I bring forth the power of light, the power of the heavens," she read aloud, "Enclosed are we within these boundaries. No evil can penetrate. It is said and it is so!"

Maggie stood before the large white candle and lit it with another small twig. She spread her arms out wide and looked up to the ceiling.

With a firm voice, she bellowed to the heavens, "Oh come all ye spirits of protection and divine energy. Come enter this space with us. Keep us from harm as ye give us the strength and wisdom to cast out the demons! Here me, oh great ancestors, and join your children in this battle between good and evil. Bring your knowledge and put it into us so that we can work on your behalf. Come... come... cccooommm-meeee!"

The room heated up to the point of almost unbearable. Brandon longed to open a window for some air but knew better than to actually do it. He had a small understanding of the ritual Maggie was performing and hummed in monotone a few long notes as a way in assisting her pull in the right vibration.

Dennis sat quietly observing. He wasn't as comfortable

with the happenings as Brandon was but he didn't argue. The entire events of the last few days were so absurd this just fit right in with it all. Tara completed her part of the ritual just as Maggie finished up.

Loud pounding on the back door filled the room.

Maggie walked cautiously over to it and called out, "Who's there?"

Her house was set far away from the road. In fact, you had to know it was there to even find it. There was no sign of a vehicle outside. They were all immediately on the alert.

"I've come for Tara" Dominic bellowed from the other side of the door.

"Dominic?" Tara gasped.

She got up and moved toward the door. Brandon grabbed her arm to stop her.

"No Lass, stay where ya are now. I'll explain later," Maggie said.

"I've come for Tara. Open up!" Dominic roared.

"Get yourself gone demon!" Maggie bellowed with equal power. "You've no business here! Be gone with ya!"

"Careful old woman. You'll mind your business, if you know what's good for you," Dominic said with a voice that belied the evil in him.

"Tara is my business, as ya well know demon," Maggie spat. "Now be gone with ya!"

Maggie wasn't deterred by Dominic's threats.

Dominic softened his tone as he tried to coax Tara to do his bidding.

"Tara, my love," he said gently, "let me in."

Tara struggled within herself. The urge to run to Dominic was acute. She longed to have him hold her and kiss her passionately like he'd done so many times before. She closed her eyes as she remembered his touches. She was lost in memories when a deep throated growl sounded from the other side of the door. It had a familiarity about it she couldn't place. It sent rivets of revulsion throughout her body. She searched her memories in an attempt to remember where she'd heard that growl before. Dominic's pounding on the door was overwhelming.

Tara screamed, "Stop it! Stop it now!"

For whatever reason it worked and all was quiet; for a moment anyway.

Maggie walked over to Tara and held her close.

"It'll be alright," she said reassuringly.

Although Dominic stopped pounding and calling for Tara, the howling was louder and more insistent. Horror flooded Tara's veins. She fought his pull and grew stronger and more in control of herself. She fell in love with a demon. She read enough of the books Maggie provided to realize how close she'd come to losing her own will. Now Dominic wanted to finish the job. What she still couldn't fathom was his reasoning for wanting her so badly.

Tara studied her companions. They were in for a long night. Dennis suffered from the strain of his wounds and would be of no help if they needed to defend themselves in any way. She remembered Liam's words. 'You have near you very dear souls who, together with you, will be able to stop the evil that has been unleashed.'

How many are out there?" Dennis asked weakly.

"Ya better get yourself off to bed now. You're fading fast on us and those wounds are opening a bit," Maggie said. "We can't fight what's outside and worry about ya as well. There's time to fill ya in later. Go on now!"

Dennis struggled to his feet at Maggie's words. Brandon grabbed his elbow and assisted him while Tara got on the other side and pulled his arm around her shoulder. Dennis fell against Tara and her knees buckled under the strain. Brandon wrapped Dennis' other arm around his shoulder to help relieve Tara of her burden. They walked into the bedroom and in flowing unison eased Dennis onto the box springs.

Tara spotted Angus resting peacefully on the mattress. She was suddenly struck with the fact that the howling hadn't disturbed him. It was odd for such a fierce protector not to respond to threats to Maggie and their home. She walked closer. He seemed too quiet. She could see no signs of breathing. She didn't dare try to rouse him in case he was just in a deep sleep. The old dog must have used a considerable amount of his strength protecting Maggie over the last few days, not to mention he'd been wounded. She decided to send Maggie in to check on him instead.

She found her loading her rifle.

"There are a lot of them out there. It looks like he's brought his army," Maggie muttered.

Brandon ran to the window. The dark of night was filled with red eyes as far as he could see. It was like a field of rubies reflecting the light of the moon.

Tara moved beside Brandon and silently took in the sea of fiery eyes and once again recalled Liam's words. 'You have near you very dear souls who, together with you, will be able to stop the evil that has been unleashed.'

Liam's words seemed incredulous. There were only three of them who were able to fight against an army of demon wolves headed by her former demon almost fiancé.

"How much ammunition do you have?" Tara asked shakily.

"Not enough to pick off that many, I'm sorry to say," Maggie replied.

She slumped as she battled defeat. Tara walked over and laid a hand on her shoulder. Maggie patted her face lovingly.

"Ya have the power," she said firmly. "If we need it, use it!"

Tara nodded in agreement, not wanting to admit that she had no idea what Maggie meant.

"Your protection spell is working at least. They're circling the house but not advancing and trying to get in." Brandon said with pleasure.

"You understand magic?" Tara asked with surprise.

"As long as we stay here, we're fine," Maggie said firmly, "but we can't stay here forever. Even though he can't come in, he can get outside and raise hell with the place. It wouldn't do to wait around and find out what he's got in mind. We need to attack."

Maggie got up and walked into the pantry room. Within minutes she was back with an old box containing two long barreled pistols. She held them lovingly.

"These were me dad's," she said nostalgically. "They're old but good enough in a pinch. Each of ya take one and aim it well. There's barely any ammunition for them." She pulled a small box of bullets from her sweater pocket and shoved it beside the guns, "That's it."

"I... I've never shot," Tara stuttered.

"Well you're about to now. Grab one and let's get started," Maggie ordered.

This wasn't a time for timidity. She positioned her body across the sink and opened the small window over the sink and poked a hole in the screen.

"Use the small windows," she barked, not offering an explanation.

Wails of beasts rang out in the night as Maggie steadily fired her rifle into the sea of eyes. It was more difficult than the night at Tara's house. The moon shone bright then. The once brilliant starry sky that guided Tara was now clouded over.

Tara joined Brandon at the back window next to the door that Dominic pounded on. Her body shook from the adrenaline that surged through her while Brandon lifted the window. She peered out into the darkness and gasped in horror.

"They're everywhere," she whispered.

Maggie called out for them to stop wasting time and shoot. Brandon took out his knife and slit the screen to make a small hole to shoot through. Tara shot into the eyes. The pistol's kick snapped her wrist but she made no mention of it. They had enough to worry about without her whining about the little things. It wasn't long before they were out of bullets and looking to Maggie for the next step. She was also running low and thinking hard about what to do next.

"We need to think of something else," she wheezed, noticeably exhausted. "There are too many of them. You're already out of bullets. If I keep shooting, I'll be out of bullets before ya know it and then we'll have no defense."

They sat in silence while they each worked out in their mind a possible solution.

"I've never seen them in the daytime, have you?" Tara asked.

"I've only seen them once before at your house, and it was dark," Brandon responded.

"They disappear at daylight. They go back to their den to rest 'till night again," Maggie pitched in. "They're creatures of the night, evil beasts that would scare themselves in the light of day." Maggie's face twisted with disgust. "They're damned ugly creatures."

Brandon was so taken aback by the look of disgust on Maggie's face and the power in her voice that he burst into laughter. When no one joined in, he apologized and awkwardly got up to stroke Sugar, who moved nervously away from him.

"'Tis going to be morning soon," Maggie muttered.

"Good!" Tara exclaimed.

"Not so good," Maggie grumbled. "They'll be working even harder to get at ya. They're running out of time." She drew a glass of water from the sink and drank it until it was empty. After releasing a loud belch and excusing herself, she walked back over to the window. "We need to trick them somehow. We need to make them think she's leaving when she's not."

Maggie paced back and forth for a bit while she wrestled for a solution in her mind. She stopped and stoked Sugar's silky neck, getting small comfort from the mare. Feeling the need to embrace her faithful Angus, Maggie searched the room for him,

"Where's Angus?" she asked.

"In all the chaos I didn't get a chance to tell you that Angus is awfully still," Tara said hesitantly. "I checked on him when we took Dennis in there but I was afraid to touch him in case I disturbed him. Maybe you should check on him yourself."

Maggie nodded and left the room. A few minutes later she came back with tears streaming down her cheeks.

"He's gone," she said softly through her tears. "My lovely companion left without me."

She lowered herself onto a chair and stared at the floor in silence. Then, with an air of determination, she wiped the tears away with her shirt sleeve and went back to where Angus lay peacefully on the mattress.

Tara rushed to help Maggie as she carried Angus and laid him on the table. She stretched him out lovingly, then walked silently into the pantry. When she returned with a long broom handle Maggie called for Brandon to join her. The two huddled together while Tara stood watching. She felt left out but kept silent, knowing it wasn't the time to ask questions. Silent tears found their way past Maggie's resolve as she worked diligently alongside Brandon to secure a broomstick to Angus' back. When done, Maggie tossed one of her shirts at Tara and ordered her to remove her own. Surprised by such a request, Tara hesitated briefly before obliging.

Brandon turned away while Tara changed tops. While she rolled up the sleeves in an attempt to make it a more comfortable fit, she watched while Brandon and Maggie put her shirt on Angus. Maggie took a pair of jeans from her closet and tied them on the lifeless dog as well.

When they were finished, Maggie's eyes echoed her sadness.

"Sit down a minute," she said to Tara. "We need to have a serious talk."

Tara sat next to Maggie who took her hand and, in a voice Tara found surprisingly gentle under the circumstances, explained her idea.

"There's nothing more precious to me in this world than Angus," she began. "He was my companion for years. He far outlived the normal life of a dog. Did I ever tell ya that?" Tara shook her head no. "He made it to thirty!" Maggie took a moment to wipe at a stray tear before continuing, "What would be even sadder than losing Angus is if that demon got to ya. You're more than the kin I know in my heart ya are. You're like me daughter." Maggie squeezed Tara's hand while Tara choked back the tears threatening to gush forth.

Tara didn't know what Maggie was about to say but she got the feeling it was something she didn't want to hear.

"Now, that mare over there," Maggie continued. "She's your love like Angus was mine, right?"

"I guess so," Tara said hesitantly. Her heart beat erratically as realization of what Maggie was leading up to set in.

"This is serious," Maggie stressed. "There's a field full of demon beasts out there and the leader is out there looking for a way to get ya away just like we're looking for a way to keep ya safe. If they get ya, you'll be like them in the end."

Tara shook her head yes. Her eyes were wide with fright as the impact of Maggie's words hit her.

"I don't know what to do," Maggie sighed. "'Tis almost daylight and they'll be pushing hard to get us out. Dominic's no longer shielding his thoughts. If they don't find a way to get ya out, they'll burn the house. Once the house is on fire, we'll have to leave and they've got us. Do ya understand?"

Tara nodded slowly as she waited to hear Maggie's idea.

"I'm sorry," Maggie hesitated. "I just can't think of anything else. We've got to make them think you're running for it. We've got to get them to chase ya so they'll waste what little time is left until the sun comes up."

Tara could hardly breathe. Her eyes darted from Angus to Sugar and back again. Maggie's idea was painfully clear.

"No," she said firmly and shook her head vehemently, "you can't."

"I just can't think of anything else. Try to understand," Maggie choked.

The old woman's limbs felt like they were full of lead as she lifted Angus off the table and carried him over to Tara's mare. Brandon followed close behind her. They propped the lifeless dog on the mare's back and used ace bandages to tie him in a sitting position. Tara had to admit that, from a distance in the dark, Angus could possibly pass as a person on horseback.

"Oh Maggie," Tara's groan came from deep within her throat.

"'Tis the horse or all of us," she said with determination. "Your brother could never make it out. Ya know that. We have no choice!"

Tara walked over to Sugar and buried her head in the mare's neck. She felt her heart was being ripped from her body. Pain seared her chest from its deepest core. Sugar nuzzled her mistress lovingly, as if to comfort her. Tara burst into tears, unable to contain them anymore.

"Maybe she'll make it Tara," Brandon whispered, hesitantly. "You never know. She's pretty fast!"

"That's true," Maggie said encouragingly. "That horse can run like the wind."

"If she runs anywhere near the way I saw Maggie run last night she'll be just fine," Brandon said jovially in an attempt to lighten the mood.

"No, no, no," Tara wailed while burying her face deep into Sugar's neck.

"Please child," Maggie's heart ached for her young friend. She wished with all her might she could think of another solution but this was all she could come up with and it was a weak solution at that.

"Tara," Brandon walked up behind her and stroked her head lightly.

As the heat of his hand penetrated her scalp, Tara slowly grew calmer. She thought of Dennis lying on the bed, weak and torn. She brought this on them and now her loving mare was going to have to pay the price. She couldn't let them do this. There had to be another way.

"No, I'm sorry, but I can't. Please take Angus off," Tara wailed. "I can't do this. I just can't."

She ripped at the bandages around Sugar's girth and Angus's lifeless form slid off. Maggie rushed to catch her life- less companion and gently lowered him to the floor.

"It was not me favorite idea, but I'm out of ideas," Mag- gie said as she cradled Angus close.

She didn't look up as she removed the rest of the ban- dages from his lifeless body and pulled the pole from his back. He was still soft and supple.

"Let me think for a minute. There has to be another way," Tara begged.

TWELVE

The howling was closer and ear piercing. Brandon went to the window and jumped back when he found himself face to face with Dominic. Dominic's eyes burned in the pre-dawn night, reflecting the anger and rage that welled within him.

"Damn!" Brandon shouted as he backed off.

Dominic pressed his face against the glass, accentuating his rage. Tara cringed to think she actually thought she could love this man. Looking at him now, she felt noting but revulsion. She hurried to the window and closed the curtains.

"I can see the pink of dawn over the trees," she said worriedly.

Something needed to be done soon. Maggie grabbed her book of spells again and quickly leafed through the pages. Without a moment's hesitation, Tara joined her. Dominic resumed pounding on the door and shouting for her to come out. Every nerve in the room was worn thin as the tension mounted. Maggie finally came to a page and stopped. She took in a deep breath as she read and then just as quickly let it out.

"What's the matter?" Tara asked, not missing how quickly Maggie lost her enthusiasm.

"It calls for fresh flowers of jasmine," Maggie wailed.

"You don't have any?" Tara exclaimed.

She was shocked. She never knew Maggie to be without any ingredient needed, no matter what page they turned to.

"I have dried jasmine inside but it calls for fresh. That's in the garden," Maggie said worriedly.

Maggie bookmarked the page before proceeding to leaf through the others. When she combed through the book without finding a suitable replacement, she went back to the bookmarked page.

"This is the only one that will work," Maggie was almost shouting to be heard over the incessant howling and pounding.

Dennis stood in the doorway of the bedroom. The chaos was overpowering. He leaned against the door frame trying to collect his wits. He felt groggy, as if he'd been drinking all night. Tara rushed to help him to a chair.

"He's feverish" she shouted as she wiped the beads of perspiration from her brother's brow.

Maggie left her book and went over to the refrigerator. She pulled out a jar of brown liquid and measured some into a small glass.

"Hold his head back and I'll pour this down him," she said. "It'll help with the fever."

Tara did as Maggie asked. The old woman practically threw the liquid down Dennis' throat. He coughed and gasped for air as he pushed the glass away from his lips. Within moments he was still again.

Dominic's pounding escalated in intensity.

"I'm going to have to go out for the jasmine. There's no other choice," Maggie quipped as she started for the door.

"You can't!" Tara screamed as she grabbed Maggie's arm to keep her from moving any further.

Maggie had grown progressively weaker as the day wore on. She couldn't explain the reasoning for this except to say that it was her time and her soul was doing its best to return to her doppelganger. Her soul memories surfaced while listening to Brandon's tale during their walk back to her little cottage. Memories were flooding back to her but so was her soul's desire to return to her other body. She prayed she could stay in this body long enough to make sure everyone was safely out of harm's way. Then she would happily return her borrowed soul. She knew all along that when Angus went, it was her time to leave as well.

"I will go!" Brandon piped in.

Both women started at Brandon. They were so engrossed in finding a solution for the problem that Tara forgot all about him. Maggie raised her hand and shook her head.

"What does it look like? Can ya tell me?" Maggie asked.

Brandon lowered his head and shook it slowly. He could hardly tell one flower from the other.

"That's what I thought," Maggie sighed.

"They're all over! They're everywhere! You'll never make it!" Tara cried.

She threw herself between Maggie and the door, trying once again to stop her.

"I'll wear my cloak," Maggie assured her. "Hopefully it will give me enough time to get the flower and get back in." She looked at Brandon and shook her head, "'Tis a shame I don't have all me powers."

Maggie moved Tara gently but firmly out of her way as she pulled a long black cloak off the hook by the door. It felt like it weighed a ton as she positioned it over her shoulders and pulled the hood up over her head.

"What will the cloak do for her?" Dennis asked weakly.

"It will make her invisible," Tara explained. "The only problem is that when the sun's rays hit it, it will sparkle. They'll be able to see it then."

She peered into the gray morning.

"If there are rays from the sun then the demons will be gone," Maggie said reassuringly.

The sun threatened to invade the darkness through the top of the trees. Dominic paced the house perimeter. He held a can of gasoline in his hands and was pouring it on the porch.

Tara watched nervously out the window.

"That son-of-a-bitch is burning the house down!"

Brandon exclaimed.

The anger in his voice superseded any fear he felt. He wanted to run out and rip the can out of Dominic's filthy hands, but common sense took over.

"Hurry, Maggie, hurry," Tara moaned as she peered at the flower bed in search of any sign of her.

Noticing Tara's searching looks, Dominic followed the direction of her eyes. A sinister smile spread across his face when he spotted grass moving under Maggie's weight. The sun beams were faint and few but enough to give off a tiny glimmer from the cloak Maggie was wearing. He raced toward her while letting out a thunderous roar.

"Maggie!" Tara screamed as Dominic plunged forward and tore her cloak off.

Maggie looked stunned as she fell to the ground. Brandon's vice grip prevented Tara from rushing out to her. She felt helpless while she listened to Maggie's cracking bones under Dominic assault. Tara witnessed her friend's struggle for air as he bore his weight down on her.

"No! Maggie!" she tried to rip her arm free from Brandon's grip.

Dennis came up behind them and secured her other arm.

"No sis. No. You can't go out there," Dennis winced from the effort of restraining his flailing sister but he stood firm and did his best. One of his wounds opened and blood oozed onto the bandage. "You can't help her. It's out of our hands. Stop... Please."

Tara watched Dominic kick Maggie's still body for signs of life. The three watched in horror, frustrated at their inability to do anything as Dominic backed away from Maggie and his demon wolves closed in. Soon the old woman was lost in the frenzy as they tore at her flesh.

She was consumed with anguish and numb with despair. Traumatized, Tara fell to the floor.

Brandon ran to the sink and vomited. His legs were

shaking and the room was spinning. His white knuckles gripped the edge of the sink while he forced back the darkness that threatened to consume him.

Only Dennis was strong enough to maintain composure. He lightly slapped his sister's cheek and said with surprising calm, "I'm sorry for all this but now isn't the time to break down." When he was sure she was lucid again, Dennis hobbled over to the window to investigate. His eyes flew wide open as he watched Dominic soaking the house with gasoline. "We're going to be burned alive if we stay in here and we'll end up like Maggie if we go out there."

"It doesn't look like there's much of an out for us," Brandon said with cold resolve as he looked from Tara to Dennis. His eyes swept the room until they rested Maggie's rifle propped against the wall. "I don't know about the two of you but neither sounds good to me." He pointed to the rifle, "I prefer going by that than by fire or them!"

Tara was wild with despair. What had she done? It was her fault Maggie was dead and it was her fault they'd soon follow. Maybe she should have listened to Maggie and put Angus on Sugar and used them as a decoy. Maggie might still be alive and them free right now; but Sugar would have died. Yes, Sugar may be a mere horse but she loved her like a human. The mare trusted and depended on her. How could she knowingly send her to her death? She was tortured with thoughts of how she sent Maggie to her death because she couldn't send her horse.

"How did it get to this?" she whispered.

"What did you say?" Brandon asked.

The seriousness of the situation mirrored back to him when he looked first at Tara's tortured face and then at Dennis as he worked to stop more blood from oozing from his recently opened wound.

Tara remembered Maggie's words. 'Ya have the power. If we need it, use it!' What was she talking about? She ran to the book Maggie left open on the table and read through the ingredients. If Maggie didn't feel they could improvise then she couldn't.

"Think, think!" Tara shouted as she repeatedly slapped her forehead with the palm of her hand.

Brandon made his way to the rifle, picked it up and walked over to Dennis.

"I know this is the way I choose to go," he said. "What about you?"

Dennis stared at the rifle in silence and then in horror at Dominic who was pouring the last of the gasoline onto the porch. The sun was on the horizon and it was easier to see the field of ugly beasts mingling amongst Maggie's remains. The gruesomeness of the situation turned his stomach. Bile filled his throat as he quickly turned away.

"No Brandon," Tara shouted. "There's another way. I feel it!"

"Well? Tell us then," Brandon said with urgent finality, "and hurry! That son-of-a-bitch lit the fire!"

Tara ran to the window to see the flames following the gasoline all around the house.

"Time's run out, Tara" Dominic bellowed with blood curdling laughter. "I was willing to marry you to gain access to the house but you let those fools stand between us. There's still time for you to come out. You don't need to die with them!"

Tara gasped, "My house?"

"You'll never find it," Brandon roared. "Whether I die or not... you'll never find it!"

"Oh, I'll find it," Dominic sneered.

"What are you talking about?" Dennis asked Brandon, but got no reply.

Tara leaned against the wall. She would worry about why Dominic wanted her house bad enough to kill them later. She frantically searched her mind for a solution. Maggie said she had the power and she inherently knew Maggie was right. It was at her fingertips but she just couldn't think what it could be. She moved to Sugar and buried her face in the mare's neck.

Her surroundings grew hazy as Sugar's telepathic words penetrated her forehead. Call upon the man, mistress. Call upon the man who helped you before.

Who was Sugar referring to? What man? The only men she could think of were in this mess with her. Who else was there? Who?

Smoke penetrated the room as the flames shot around the house. Dennis struggled to keep his coughing from disturbing his wounds.

"You two can stick around if you want," Brandon said with conviction. "I have no desire to go this way! I'm using this!" He reached over for the box of ammunition to load the rifle.

Suddenly Tara remembered. She knew what Sugar was trying to say. She recalled Liam's message. 'We are in hopes this can be done without the need of our assistance. If not, you are to simply call... we cannot interfere unless you ask... Say my name three times and help will be available.'

With a voice as loud as she could possibly muster, Tara cried "Help Liam! Please help! Liam! Liam! Liam!"

The room instantly filled with light and the smoke disappeared. Brandon dropped the rifle and stared with disbelief. Tara ran to the window. Demon wolves were exploding everywhere. She peered through the receding smoke and flames and watched Dominic shift himself into the same wolf she encountered on the roadside. Liam stood before him with outstretched arms while the wolf slowly transformed back into Dominic's form and he laid twisting and writhing while he fought off the energy destroying him. Within a matter of minutes, the field was empty, the fire was out and Liam was gone.

Tara, Dennis, and Brandon stood in a room so quiet a pin dropping could be easily heard.

"What just happened?" Dennis broke the silence as he stood in disbelief looking at his bloodless bandages. "My wounds are healed. How could that be?"

"A miracle," Tara said with relief. She rushed over to Sugar and hugged her tightly. "Thank you. Thank you for reminding me. Thank you."

"Let's get out of here," Brandon said softly.

Dennis walked over to Tara and pulled her close, "Let's go home."

****

Dennis and Brandon returned that afternoon with the police to retrieve what remained of poor Maggie. They hadn't told the truth, since they knew no one would believe them. Maggie's body was in shreds so the police wrote the report up stating she was the victim of a wild animal attack. After all, there were multiple reports from around the county about sightings of a strange looking wolf pack. It must have made its way to the old woman's house. The singed circle around the house was passed off as some queer ritual. It was no secret she was a bit odd and there were also rumors of her practicing witch craft.

Tara went straight to bed. By the time she awoke, three days had passed and her Aunt Eva was adjusting her covers. Tara pulled her close and hugged her so tight the woman gasped for air. Hearing her struggle, Tara loosened her grip but didn't let go. Eva adjusted herself so she could lie comfortably next to her niece and the two of them remained there in silence; eventually falling into a gentle slumber.

By the time they awoke the house was full of activity. Eva jumped up to investigate, but motioned Tara to stay put. She wanted her niece to take it easy for just a bit longer. Dennis had confided all. What he couldn't tell, Brandon did. It was obvious to Eva that a bond had formed between the two men during the horror of the last few days.

The thought of her niece enduring such trauma and having to watch her best friend die was crushing but she did her best to hide her feelings and be the rock for them all to lean on. Her nephew had been through enough and shouldn't be expected to do anything more and she was far too unfamiliar with Brandon to place any demands on him. Besides, even though she didn't know him well it was clear that he was also severely affected by the ordeal they'd endured. How could he not be?

Brandon decided to hang around for a few days to make sure Tara and Dennis were fine. He also admitted that he was still a little shaken and not quite up to facing the world. Eva and Dennis understood completely.

The better part of a week passed before Tara came out of her room. Still not up to talking to anyone, she snuck away to the stable. The fall air was crisp and moist. It felt like the upcoming rainstorm could easily turn into snow if the temperature dropped just a few more degrees. Her mare snorted puffs of moist air as she watched her approach. Tara made her way into the stall with the intent of doing a little cleaning. She was sure neither Dennis nor Eva had taken readily to the task and did only what they absolutely needed to. To her surprise, the place was cleaner than she ever knew it to be.

"I hope you don't mind, but I took the liberty while you were resting. It gave me something to do," Brandon's voice came from the shadows.

Tara searched and could barely make out the outline of his lean body in the recesses of the building.

"Why are you lurking in the shadows?" she asked nervously.

"I'm not lurking. I thought I was alone and was resting," he replied. "Had I realized you were coming I'd have greeted you in the open. I didn't mean to frighten you."

"Its fine," she said quickly, "and... thanks. You did a better job than I've ever done."

Tara could feel the tension slowly leaving her.

"I grew up around horses," Brandon said. "I find the work therapeutic. I have a method. I will show you sometime if you like."

Although his words where friendly and casual, his body ached with anxiety. She was so beautiful and vibrant, even after all that happened. He longed to hold her close and tell her how sorry he was for her pain. He wanted to tell her how lovely she was. If she would only remember.

He'd left her nothing to do, but Tara picked up a rake and started cleaning anyway.

Brandon stood heavy hearted and watched her for a while before making his way up the path to the house. He'd stayed on as a guest longer than planned while he waited to see her. There was no reason to stay any longer. If the shock of what happened didn't jolt her memories free then nothing would. It was time to leave. He sought out Dennis and Eva to thank them for their hospitality. Dennis tried to talk him into staying a bit longer but he insisted it was time to go. He refused an offer from Dennis to take him to town; instead, insisting on calling a cab.

The cab was scheduled to arrive at seven which left time for dinner. Eva quickly threw together a light meal and pulled a bottle of wine from the wine rack. She wanted to make Brandon's parting meal as pleasant as possible. As they sat at the table, conversation was difficult. Each one wanted to say something but the words wouldn't come.

Dennis finally broke the silence, "I wish you would stick around a bit longer."

Brandon shook his head, "I'll swing back off and on."

"I hope you mean that," Dennis said in earnest. "I'm serious man."

"I promise," Brandon smiled as they all clanked their glasses together in a toast to solidify his vow.

****

Tara sat at the window looking out at the stars. It grew dark so early now that fall was ending. It couldn't be more than six o'clock. She declined joining them for Brandon's parting dinner, feigning a headache. Eva brought her a food tray and she sat nibbling at it now. She thought of Maggie and wondered if she would ever find peace in her heart again. The loss was intense. She wanted to ride Sugar to Maggie's house and find her there sitting on the porch petting Angus, like she had so many times before.

She found herself wandering the house and settling in the upstairs den. She pulled Maggie's book from the bookshelf, holding its bulk to her chest lovingly. It smelled like Maggie. She filled her lungs with its scent. It was all she had left of her dear friend. Opening up the pages, she landed on the section of angels. Surely such a pure soul of Maggie was one now.

"Her soul has returned to her other incarnation. Fear not, for she is happy," Liam said warmly.

Tara turned to find Liam standing in the shadows of the room. There was no glowing ball and he didn't look as bright as he had the other times he'd appeared to her. He glimmered soft and warm.

"You're wondering about my brightness?" Liam smiled at Tara's surprised look, "Yes, I can hear your thoughts. It is simple. I am standing amongst the shadows of time. It is the plane between times as you know it. It is the space where all travel is done. I have not fully come to you and not fully left where I have been. I spent time with Maggie before her soul re-settled. She asked that I tell you she is happy and whole. She wishes you would retrieve her family secrets from her home before they are discovered and taken by others. She says you are to continue with your studies. There is a will to be read in the safe deposit box at the bank. She has willed all her earthly belongings to you. It is her desire that you find peace within yourself and do your best to remember who you are and find what you came for."

She stepped toward him hesitantly but he remained motionless. Clearing her throat, she asked, "Can I enter the shadows in time? Is that possible?"

What Tara asked to do was something very few humans were able to do. It was possible, of course, but most choose to die and reincarnate rather than brave the shadows of time. Liam was silent for several moments while he contemplated his response.

He looked at her with compassionate warmth as he replied, "If you can think it, believe in it and trust in it, anything is possible." As he slowly faded away his words echoed softly through the room, "Remember, I am always near."

ONE

Flames engulfed the cottage and taunted the leaves of the old apple tree, forcing its sap to the surface to help ease the scattered damage to the charred bark. The hot, dry air seared her lungs. She'd never experienced heat of this nature. Her skin hurt to touch. She could see the evilness in Dominic's eyes as he prowled the parameter of the dwelling. His bellowing pierced through the chaos, "I want to you Tara. If I can't have your body, I'll have your soul!"

Tara's firelight curls fell over her shoulders and down her back in wild abandonment as she shook free memories of that horrible, fateful night. Sliding her hands up the sleeves of her oversized lamb's wool sweater she hugged her tall, slender body against the chill both from the air and her thoughts.

Leaning her head against the window pane, her dark green eyes peered at the blanket of frantic white snowflakes as they billowed toward barely visible outbuildings. The howling gales of winter echoed throughout the rolling Pennsylvania valley with a resemblance of a collective of musical instruments paying homage to old man winter while they shook the one-hundred-eighty-year-old house; rattling its windows with such force that one might expect the antique dwelling to be swept into the Land of Oz.

The nor'easter had arrived with a vengeance, showing no mercy for the impuissant inhabitants of the land. She'd focused so hard on preparing the grand old house for the oncoming winter that the equally grand stable hadn't received the attention to insure its strength for a season of storms such as this.

The storm made it easy for her to come to terms with her decision to find a handyman to finish the needed repairs. She filled her lungs with the crisp air that managed to find its way through her newly caulked windows and hoped the outbuildings were sturdy enough to make it to spring in one piece; after which she'd give them the attention they required.

Her daydream was so real, her lungs actually felt singed. She drew in as much cooling air as she could one more time and then released it slowly, focusing on the light mist that formed from the moist warmth of her breath on the cold window pane.

She was always active and outgoing. Finding herself snowed in with limited connection to the outside world for over a week took its toll on her mood. It gave her far too much time to think. It ripped at her soul to know that because of her and her stupidity in summoning the dark side -followed by her poor choice in men- many had suffered loss and heartache.

She walked over to the large, overstuffed horse-hair sofa she recently had restored and snuggled under the thick multi-colored afghan her Aunt Eva gifted her at Christmas. The roaring fire in the newly renovated fireplace illuminated the rustic red bricks that spoke of days gone by. She missed her aunt and was eager for her next visit. Her loneliness was accentuated not only by her missing Eva's vibrancy, but Dennis was on vacation down south and her father had called her last minute full of excitement about his archeological find and begged to be excused from the holidays because he didn't dare abandon the dig and risk vandalism. Tara understood, but was still saddened by his absence.

The warmth emanating from the dancing flames struggled to evade the draw of the chimney that permitted it to merely hover within feet of the open hearth, leaving the rest of the room prey to the icy air that crept steadily through the badly insulated walls and windows. The dilapidated steam radiators that were installed throughout the house soon after their invention provided little assistance. She stood up and pushed the sofa closer toward the fire, being careful not to get so close that a stray spark might damage its rich, newly applied tapestry upholstery. Resuming her spot under the afghan, she passed the dismal afternoon hours in cozy slumber.

The setting sun crept over the distant mountain top before Tara roused herself from her blissful snooze. The fire needed attention. She debated whether to add more wood and stoke it back to its former level or let it die out for the night. The house had eighteen fireplaces and, although she enjoyed the ambience of her downstairs study, surely, she could find a room more protected from the outdoor elements and start a warming fire there. Deciding it was best to close the room off until its leaks were tended to, she pushed the glowing remnants of heat under a pile of thick, lifeless ashes and felt the last hint of warmth trickle away. Satisfied, she rubbed her upper arms against the impending cold of the night yet to come and left the room.

The antique grandfaher clock that stood regally at the far end of the second-floor hallway chimed six o'clock. It was time for Sugar's nightly feed.

She pulled on her heaviest hooded sweatshirt and thick insulated socks, followed by her goose down parka, insulated gloves, fur lined rubber boots, thick woolen neck scarf, and a pair of snowmobile goggles. True warmth spread through her chilled body for the first time all day. She was sorry to have to ruin it by going out into the cold, but she had responsibilities that were unavoidable.

Pushing the solid oak exterior door -that she was told was an original part of the house- open against the elements that were raising havoc wasn't an easy feat. Gusts of pelting ice mixed with snow still dominated the atmosphere. Pulling her woolen neck scarf over her nose, she plunged forward. It took all her strength to forge her way down the one-hundred-yard path to the stable. She could hear the crunch beneath her well protected feet as she broke through the mid-calf high seemingly endless sea of crusted snow.

Even with all the layers of warmth on her body, she felt the cold. Her moist breath left tiny frozen crystals along her lips and in her nostrils. She focused her flashlight in all directions while she checked for unwanted creatures lingering in the night, a habit she developed after her encounter with Dominic's demon beasts.

Time dragged as she plunged her way through the blinding blanket of white. When she finally reached the stable, she stared in breathless dismay at the amount of ice and snow that needed to be removed before she could slide the door far enough to pass her slender body through.

The sudden realization that she left the snow shovel on the opposite side of the door resulted in one of the loudest wails of frustration she could recall ever emitting. The urge to kick the door was overwhelming, but her legs were held hostage in the ever-deepening heavy snow. The best she could do was lean her body against the side of the building and slam her heavily mitted fist against it. Sugar's whinny had a calming effect on her and she relaxed enough to think how to get into the stable.

Thin, icy tree branches lightly brushed her head as a gust of wind whisked a thin layer of the tree's burden off into the night. She would have found the spindly boughs of an ancient apple tree, that were laden with a thick coat of snow atop icicles that reached low to the ground, wonderfully marvelous to gaze upon under better circumstances. Wiping the excess snow from her face, she studied the tree and its position to the building. Its thick trunk indicated it was much older than the stable.

The thud of the branches scraping against the wooden door to the hay loft added percussion to the melodious whistling of the wind. She shone her flashlight to inspect the situation as best she could. Even laden with snow, the branches looked sturdy enough. If she was careful, she could climb up and enter through the loft. Under the best of circumstances Tara would have been hesitant to climb a tree, but she saw no other option. Once inside she'd be sure to grab that darn shovel and keep it in a place of easy access.

Tucking her trusty flashlight in the inside pocket of

her coat, she wiped the melting snow from her goggles and gripped the lower branch of the ancient and gnarled apple tree.

"Here goes nothing!" she shouted into the night.

It took a moment for her eyes to adjust to the lack of the flashlight's helpful beam, but soon she was maneuvering with confidence. Although her slender frame was in prime physical condition, heaving her heavily clad body out of the deep snowy wells that sucked at her legs like quicksand felt almost unattainable. The exertion left her body wet and clammy with perspiration. She felt laden with damp, cumbersome, and smelly fabric. She was just about to give up when she found reserved strength to pull her out of the snow and make her way from one branch to the next.

Now that she was up the tree, the door was further from the branch than it looked when she was on the ground assessing things. She hadn't realized the actual extent of the ice on the branches either. She was higher than she thought she'd be when she first started this venture and, from her present position the branches felt dangerously feeble. The gnarled and rickety limb that she just hoisted her weight from threatened to rot away from the ancient, gnarled tree trunk. The new branch that she balanced carefully on felt like it might be a little too thin to hold her much longer. Looking closer, she realized that the old fruit tree was actually in need of serious TLC. She cursed the darkness. If she'd accessed the situation in the daylight, she wouldn't have climbed the tree to begin with.

As she stretched her body as much as she could, she caught a glimpse through the pelting snow into the endless darkness below. Climbing back down the prime candidate for the wood pile looked even more precarious than making her way to the loft door from her not-so-sturdy perch. She grabbed the frame of the loosely hinged door and from a crouched position, flung her body hard against it. It all happened as if she's performed a choreographed stunt in a movie. Her body hit its mark and the door flung open. She landed unceremoniously onto a pile of old, dusty hay.

Bits of sharp, dust riddled straw sent her into a fit of sneezing as her nose did its best to cleanse her nasal cavities, stopping only when it succeeded in flushing the majority of it out and leaving her sadly in need of a handkerchief. Rummaging through her pockets and coming up empty handed, she shrugged and used the sleeve of her down jacket; shuddering at her own actions. She grabbed a fist full of snow from the door frame and wiped her sleeve with it.

The ache on her rib cage reminded her of the location of her flashlight. Wincing, she reached in and pulled it out by its thick barrel and clicked on the beam. She'd been in this part of the loft only once and had never really taken the time to inspect it closely. Sugar's quarters were on the far end of the building. Shining the flash light's beam through swirling particles of dust and bits of hay that rode the occasional gusts of winter through the loft door, she was surprised to come upon a group of portraits leaning against the interior wall.

Looking closer, she saw they were of people dressed in eighteen and nineteenth century attire. Interestingly, one man was in a confederate solder's uniform. She was no expert, but after a more in-depth examination of the paintings, she was certain that they weren't recently painted. They were surprisingly well preserved, but clearly quite old. Tara felt certain the artist managed to portray a very strong likeness to the people in the paintings. She wasn't sure how she knew this. It was just something she felt.

The sound of her mare's stomping below brought Tara back to matters at hand. Making certain to securely latch the loft door, she searched for the ladder that would take her to the main floor and carefully picked her way down it. Once her footing found the concrete base of the stable she relaxed. She was on familiar ground now and, although the flashlight came in handy, she could actually accomplish what she needed to do without light if the situation called for it. Fortunately, the electricity hadn't been interrupted by the brutal storm and she was able to light up her surroundings with a flip of the switch.

Sugar's excitement in seeing her was barely contained. There had been no telepathic communication between them since the night of Maggie's brutal murder, but there was no need for Tara to understand her four-legged friend's greeting. The mare was happy to see that her owner and care taker had arrived and her needs would be tended to.

The mare's part of the old stable was fairly well protected from the storm. Tara lowered the scarf from her face and removed her thick mittens so her hands could maneuver more comfortably. The heat of Sugar's breath as she nuzzled her affectionately was a welcome sensation. Working as quickly as she could, she refreshed the water bucket, put a wedge of hay in the hay rack, a scoop of grain in the feed bucket and made certain the mare's blanket was secure before she reached for the pitch fork to remove the soiled hay.

She thought nothing of the piercing cold on her cheeks and continued pitching hay, hoping to be finished quickly and get back to the comfort of a hot bath and a snug blanket. When the cold grew bone chilling, she couldn't ignore it any longer. This part of the stable was too well protected for this type of cold to be assaulting her. She checked around for its source. Her breath caught in her throat and her chest constricted as she found herself staring into the large, brown eyes of the old man who hadn't appeared in months.

Unlike the other times when he was there and then gone almost as quickly, he stood zombie-like and as three-dimensionally opaque as any human would be. The only thing differentiating him from Tara was the hazy glow around his body. Every nerve stood at attention while she debated what to do. Running away was her first inclination, but a ghost could pop in and out whenever and wherever it desired, so running would be futile. Besides, how far could she possibly get in that blizzard? She longed for Maggie. Maggie would know what to do and Maggie wouldn't be so frightened.

With trembling hands, Tara moved the pitch fork in front of her and continued to clean Sugar's stall. Perhaps, if she ignored him, he'd go away. Sugar scraped her hoofs and snorted her disapproval. The air bursting from her nostrils created tiny clouds that floated into nothingness. The ghost wasn't going to go away, but it wasn't saying anything either. As if seeing a ghost wasn't frightening enough, his staring was creepy.

She was about to confront him when he uttered "Lucy", in an almost inaudible voice that held a distinct and thick brogue and then faded into nothingness.

Tara was dumbfounded. It took a stinging slap across her face by Sugar's coarse tail to bring her back to reality. Her body trembled, but at least the air warmed up to the point where her breath was barely visible. She recalled the book Maggie gave to her explained why the air got so cold when a ghost appeared, but she couldn't remember the details. She'd forgotten a lot of the teachings Maggie had worked so hard to instill within her along the way. They were locked up tight in the recesses of her mind; too painful to remember, for by remembering them she remembered Maggie. She shook her head. Did the reasons why the air got cold when a ghost appeared really matter after all was said and done? She thought not.

"It's for the best," she said aloud, "I don't need to know all of that mumbo jumbo. Look at what it got me. Not to mention what it got Maggie. It's just as well that I forget it all."

She hurried to complete her chores. The encounter with the ghost was quickly pushed into the back of her mind, along with the other memories she wanted to diminish and, hopefully, forget.

TWO

The storm ceased sometime during the early hours just before sunrise, leaving behind it mini mountains of icy snow to be removed before her home could run at its normal pace.

Tara sighed. Winters in Manhattan were so much easier. She couldn't have imagined such burdensome weather and was therefore not totally prepared for it. She was grateful for the good sense she exercised in following Maggie's suggestion to purchase the small tractor with a snow plow attachment. A cold reminder of her friend, the valuable piece of equipment was left dormant since the day it was delivered.

Today it would make its debut.

She'd programmed her coffee maker prior to going to bed and wafts of the dark liquid's rich aroma lured her out from beneath the warm security of her goose down comforter. She hated the cold and often wondered why her crazy ancestors settled in the north. Even if they had come from a cold climate, surely, they could have acclimated to the warmth of the south had they given it a chance. She dreaded the air that awaited her outside her covers. She'd have stayed in it all day if she hadn't had duties and responsibilities. They forced her to brave the brisk air of the large, poorly insulated rooms of the great house.

She'd just reveled in her first sip of coffee when the telephone rang.

She rushed to answer it, hoping it was Dennis calling to tell her he was on his way. He'd urged her to join him on his vacation down south, but she neither felt the inclination to go, nor was she as free as she was when she boarded Sugar elsewhere. Now, if she wanted to go somewhere for any length of time she had to hire someone to look after her mare, her kittens, and her house. She wasn't up to entrusting people she didn't know with her most precious possessions. After her nightmare with Dominic, her trust level was exceedingly low.

Looking at the after effects of the horrendous storm, she wondered if leaving Manhattan was the wisest thing. She wasn't a farm girl and didn't profess to have any skill with something as formidable as a tractor and snow plow. The thought of having to sit on the mini-monster and maneuver it through the thick blanket of heavy, crystallized precipitation that went on for as far as the eye could see was horrifically intimidating. She fervently hoped that it was Dennis calling to tell her he'd returned early from his trip.

"So, how goes it out there in no man's land?" Mitch's sarcastic tone of voice that accompanied the equally sarcastic remark grated on her already frazzled nerves. "I understand you had a whopper of a storm last night. I just called to see how you survived it."

"I hoped you were Dennis," Tara grumbled.

"I see you're your usual sunny self in the morning. No coffee yet?" he sighed.

Having her rudeness so clearly pointed out startled Tara into realizing just how much she'd changed since she moved into her beautiful country estate.

As if reading her mind, Mitch continued, "You know, the Tara O'Shea that I knew and loved would have never been so curt and thoughtless, no matter how she felt inside. She was always the epitome of social etiquette. I'm not sure how I feel about the Tara you've become since you moved to the country. I think the hustle and bustle of Manhattan produced a much more amiable female."

"I'm sorry. I'm not feeling all that great today," she said earnestly. After a moment's silence she added, "I hear you're in love. Congrats."

"I am and thanks. I want you to meet her. I think you

two will get along great. She has a lot of qualities you'd like. It's like you two could be sisters or something," Mitch said and then quickly added, "That's not why I'm with her. I love her for who she is. In fact, I asked her to marry me."

"I..." she started before he continued and interrupted her.

"I thought we'd pop out to your place this weekend," he said brightly. "Dennis should be back by then, right?"

Tara groaned inwardly. The last thing she wanted to do was entertain her former love and his new love, but things had smoothed out between them enough to make being around him tolerable and she didn't want them to revert back to the tenseness that dominated their interaction after they broke up. She regretted the fact that Dennis was good friends with him. She saw no way out of playing hostess to the new lovers.

"You're more than welcome," she lied.

Although the sun lit up the thick white blanket of endless crystallized sea, the air was still brutal. Mitch's voice faded into the background as she focused on the cold that consumed her room. There were some portions of the house that she hadn't yet managed to protect against the elements, but this particular room was one of the very first to be renovated. She watched the first flakes of snow fall with the illusion that she'd be warm and snug in this room at least.

The bitter cold she experienced now was disheartening. What could she have missed? What didn't get patched, insulated, caulked or weather-stripped? The tickling of the back of her neck as her hair stood at attention alerted her that she wasn't alone in the room. These feelings only happened when something not human appeared. It was an explanation for the cold, at least. She wasn't sure if she should be happy or unhappy about it.

Not up to facing whatever it was, she closed her eyes and prayed it would go away while Mitch continued with his recapitulation of the events leading up to his meeting and falling in love with Alana. He rambled on, completely unaware that his audience was only half listening. She finally let her eyes comb the room for the intruder. It was only a matter of seconds before she spotted him.

The old ghost was back.

She wasn't sure if ghosts were telepathic, but she sent him a message to leave anyway. Whether he heard her thoughts or simply felt it was time to go, she wasn't certain. Whatever the case, she gave a sigh of relief as she watched him fade away.

Just as his shape reached the point of being barely visible, she heard a faint "Lucy" in the same thick brogue that was spoken the night before. She had no idea why this ghost would be calling her Lucy and for the present she had no desire to find it out.

"Does that work for you?" Mitch's question brought her back to reality.

"Does what work for me?" she asked.

"I said," Mitch's impatience was clearly noted in his tone, "we can be there about five o'clock on Saturday."

"I'll make a pot roast," she said as she tried to reign in her focus.

"Sounds good," he replied.

Without seeing if Mitch had more to add to the conversation or even politely saying 'good-bye', Tara returned the receiver to its cradle and sat down to drink her coffee. Who was this ghost and why did he keep coming around? She didn't like it. She didn't like it one bit!

She missed Maggie.

Tara had only just started allowing herself brief glimpses into her memories of her time with Maggie. Little by little the shock of Maggie's brutal death at the hands of Dominic and his evil beasts was ebbing away and she was able to feel again. She could finally grieve properly. Now seemed like a good time to cry, so she did it with gusto. Since there was no one in the house with her except her rapidly growing kittens, there was no one to stop her; no one to comfort her; no one to care. Even though she knew this, she still imagined Maggie walking in her usual unannounced way through the door to linger in the recesses of her mind.

****

Tara fidgeted with her long firelight curls as she watched the tall, slender form of the future Mrs. Mitchell Longworth -better known as Alana- slide gracefully out of the late model Jaguar he'd miraculously maneuvered down the long, tree lined driveway she'd made a pathetic attempt to plow. The enormous fur hood hugging Alana's face and neck made it impossible to tell if she was a blonde, brunette, or redhead, but Tara lay dibs that Mitch's goddess was a blonde. Her breath caught in her throat as the woman looked in her direction. Mitch hadn't done his future wife justice. He'd declared her beauty over and over, but it always seemed that perhaps his vision was clouded by love. She could see now that it wasn't. Alana had to be the most beautiful woman Tara had ever laid eyes on.

Doing her best to arrange a few stray strands of hair with her suddenly clumsy fingers and wishing she'd chosen an outfit other than jeans and oversized hand knitted cotton sweater that hung loosely over her slender hips, she ran to the doorway to welcome her guests.

"Damn, it's cold!" Mitch said as he stomped the snow from his boots. He kissed Tara on the cheek and pulled his fiancé forward for a proper introduction. "I want you to meet Alana. Alana, this is Tara."

Alana was surprised when Tara showed no signs of recognition. Dominic had spoken truth. Alana could always tell when Lucy was lying. She'd clearly lost so much of her memory she actually thought herself to be Tara O'Shea. Well, at least she remembered the O'Shea.

"Welcome," Tara said with a little too much exuberance.

She hoped her words came across sincerer than she felt as she hustled her guests into the house and out of the bitter cold.

Mitch wasted no time in shedding his coat and scarf.

"I can't believe how fast this weather came upon us," he said. "One day I was enjoying a balmy fall day and then I woke up and there was snow everywhere!"

Tara furrowed her brows as she listened to Mitch ramble on. He seemed nervous. Was he worried she hadn't approved of his fiancé? What did her opinion matter anyway? Was there something about her that would make her not approve? She looked from Mitch to Alana for a clue.

"Your home is lovely," Alana said.

The words glided off Alana's tongue and past her perfectly aligned, pearly teeth just as gracefully as she'd glided out of the car. Tara was duly intimidated.

"It's a diamond in the rough," Tara managed to say, "but I'm excited about the end result. I have a vision in my mind of how it should be. I want to restore it as much as I can to its original condition."

"Really," Alana mused as she walked to the banister and caressed it admiringly. "I suppose that would be nice. Some people would take a fine structure like this and bring it up to date; modernize it. I think the old fashion is still beautiful." Alana flashed a smile that would melt a snowman in seconds, "Very beautiful."

Tara held her arms out to receive Alana's coat and hung it on the antique coat tree that came with the house. She only recently got it back from the furniture restorer she discovered while looking for a handyman. His work was excellent and his rates were surprisingly reasonable.

"I agree," Tara said awkwardly. "I put in a few new windows and an intercom system, but otherwise I'm doing my best to keep it as real as I can. Can I get you something hot to drink... coffee... tea... hot chocolate?"

"Brandy?" Mitch said with amusement.

"Can she drink?" Alana whispered to Mitch.

"Brandy it is," Tara replied, choosing to ignore Alana's question.

Tara suddenly regretted telling Dennis he didn't have to rush over. He'd sounded so exhausted from his fun in the sun that she insisted he relax and not rush coming to her house, but she really didn't want to be left entertaining his good friend -who was also her ex-boyfriend- and his gorgeous catty fiancé on her own. She was extremely uncomfortable.

At one time, Maggie would have been here with her; her bubbly personality dominating the room. The wave of sadness that consumed Tara didn't go unnoticed by her guests. Mitch and Alana exchanged looks with raised brows.

"Is everything okay? Are you okay? You seem sad," Mitch said with gentle concern; a factor that didn't pass by Alana.

He touched Tara's elbow lightly, adding to her sadness as it brought back memories of the good old days.

A dark cloud swept over Alana's brilliant blue eyes while she contemplated the exchange of emotional familiarity between Mitch and Tara. Their touch was too familiar for her not to question if there was more between these two than the good friends Mitch claimed they were.

Alana was gorgeous and she knew it, but Lucy was a beauty in her own right and could potentially pose a threat to her position with Mitch and her plans. Familiar feelings of rivalry surfaced. She wouldn't let Lucy beat her, memory loss or not. She needed to act quickly. Inching closer to Mitch, she touched his forearm seductively.

"Mitch, honey," she purred. "Perhaps our hostess is just tired. I mean... look at her, she looks worn out and it's no wonder. If what you tell me is true, she cares for this big place all by herself."

Mitch didn't catch Alana's undertone, but Tara certainly did. She would have been offended if Alana hadn't been so right. She was exhausted, but not from maintaining the place.

She was tired from life. She felt like a bedraggled mop after what she went through. She probably did look as bad as she felt, but for a perfect stranger to say such a thing to her host was both appalling and insulting.

Tara locked eyes with Alana. Each woman did her best to relay her position with expression. Tara wanted Alana to know that she was on to her phoniness and Alana wanted it to be clear that Tara wouldn't beat her on anything.

Tara sighed. Leave it to Mitch to bring a viper into her home. Hadn't she been through enough?

Their silent exchange passed right past Mitch without notice.

"Well, hell Tara! Why don't you get some help out here?" Mitch asked as he twisted his head to look through the doorway of the parlor. "Where's that old woman who's always here? Dennis told me she's been good company for you. What's her name again?"

"Maggie," Tara said softly. Tears surprised everyone as they slid down Tara's cheeks while she choked out the words, "She's dead."

Mitch was horrified.

"Tara. I'm sorry," he said apologetically. "Dennis never said... I didn't know... Dead? When? How?"

"A few months ago," Tara said as she sniffed back the tears. She wiped at her moist cheeks with her sleeve, not caring about the impression such an unsophisticated action made on Alana and added, "I'm really not up to talking about it."

"Sure," Mitch replied. He put his arms around his former love and held her close; ignoring the jealous snorts emitted by his future wife, who remained close at his side. "I'm sorry I brought it up. I didn't know. I'm sorry. I just didn't know."

"It's okay," Tara assured him.

Her voice was muffled as she buried her face deep into Mitch's chest. It was some time since she felt the strong support of a human hug and she wasn't anxious to give it up. Knowing that his catty bitchy fiancé was standing nearby and wasn't happy with what she witnessed, Tara kept her eyes closed to avoid having to face the consequences of her actions for just a little longer.

Alana snarled inwardly. Mitch's display of concern for Lucy made her stomach turn. She smiled inwardly about the fact that she'd deliberately destroyed Dennis' letter telling Mitch what happened to Maggie. He told the whole sordid story of how Dominic tried to marry his sister in order to get possession of the house and find something. Fortunately, they never found out what that something was and poor, poor Lucy was far too traumatized to use her brain and think to look for it. She didn't doubt the whiny thing would tell the story to Mitch during their visit, but she planned on finding the crystal key and getting out of there before Lucy knew what happened.

Mitch interpreted Alana's thoughtful scowl as disapproval of his attempt to comfort Tara. He knew that in spite of her almost overwhelming beauty, Alana was a jealous female. Tara's beauty could easily rival Alana's. Hugging her was asking for trouble. He shrugged his shoulders and gave a look of chagrin, hoping to lighten the situation as much as he could as he gently pushed Tara away. To his surprise and relief, it worked and Alana's scowl gradually transformed into a broad smile.

Tara pulled herself together.

"Let me show you to your room so you can get comfortable," she said as she directed her attention to Alana. "Are you hungry? I made pot roast."

Alana sniffed the air and said in a sickly-sweet tone, "It smells wonderful."

Tara flashed one of the warmest smiles she could muster in Alana's direction, hoping to smooth over the tension. She had no idea why such a gorgeous woman would be jealous of her, but it was written all over her face; if only for a moment. As she guided them to their room, she was grateful her home was so large. She'd decided to put them in a room at the far end of the house that had only recently been furnished and prepared for guests rather than her normal guest rooms, which were closer to her own. She wanted to have Alana's negative jealousy as far away from her as possible while she was in the vulnerable state of sleep.

While passing the full-length mahogany trimmed mirror that was centered along the wide, elaborate landing that attached her quarters to the guest quarters, she caught a glimpse of herself. Alana was right. She looked worn out. There was nothing for her beautiful guest to be jealous about in this house, nothing at all.

Suddenly Tara regretted the bad start they'd had gotten off to. After all, it wasn't as if she wanted Mitch for herself. As for the woman's phoniness... well, it was probably standard in beautiful women. Beauty could be a powerful tool when dealing with men such as Mitch. Tara could hardly hold Alana's use of what nature bestowed against her.

Alana walked up behind Tara and stood looking at their reflection. Tara gasped as she realized how closely they resembled each other. Mitch was right. They could be sisters; with Alana being the prettier one. She watched as Alana adjusted a few stray hairs with the grace of a debutante and sighed. Tara craved female companionship and she wanted to get to know the future wife of her former love. Well, it wasn't too late. Perhaps, after everyone rested and dined she'd try to mend the fence between them before it got even worse.

****

Dinner went smoother than Tara imagined. After a hot shower and short nap, Alana's mood was more amiable.

She expressed a deep appreciation for the old house. Thrilled to have someone share her passion for everything vintage, Tara happily accommodated her with a tour. The two used their time alone to break through the icy chill that started their relationship and get to know each other a little better.

Tara showed Alana every nook and cranny of her grand abode. Alana took in everything like she was burning it to memory.

Mitch, never an admirer of anything old, opted to relax in the den by the fireplace with a good scotch whiskey in his hand.

Tara found the amount she had in common with Alana remarkable. They not only looked similar, but had similar tastes in just about everything, including men.

The hours passed quickly and before she knew it, it was time to say good-night. Mitch and Alana's trip over snowy and sometimes icy roads in a sports car was tedious and tense. The exhaustion from the trip combined with full bellies, alcohol, and a blazing fireplace, had practically put them to sleep in their chairs. Tara felt a little guilty for not considering their situation earlier and waiting until they could no longer disguise their yawns and droopy eyelids before suggesting they call it a night. Since she'd already shown them to their room and Alana now knew her way around the house almost as well as she did, Tara opted to remain downstairs to tidy up before retiring.

Feeling wonderfully cozy and satisfied with the way the evening went, she kissed the couple on their cheeks and bid them good-night. It was good to have life in the house again. She'd missed the companionship more than she realized.

Humming a non-descript tune, she picked up their glasses and the Mikasa snack dish that at one time sported an array of gourmet crackers and cheeses, but now, thanks to Mitch, had barely a crumb left thanks, and headed for the kitchen sink. She would wash them in the morning.

The cold chill down her back practically took her breath away. She didn't need to look around to know what was going on.

He was back.

Her exhaustion combined with the frustration over the appearing and disappearing of the resident ghost -mixed with the generous amount of brandy she'd consumed during the evening- gave her an abnormal sense of bravery.

"Who are you and what do you want!" she demanded while she continued to pick up the dishes. When she received no response, she continued, "If you aren't going to tell me, then just go away. I'm tired of your tedious visits. Speak or get out."

"Lucy," the ghost whispered.

"Who's Lucy?" she asked impatiently.

Tara set the glass she just rinsed off on the drain of the sink and turned to face the semi-transparent old man. As she did so, he faded away, but not before he issued a warning.

"Come home... danger," he said in a barely audible whisper.

Tara stood, motionless, as she stared at the spot where the old ghost had appeared. She had no clue what he could possibly be saying. She tried to remember the other times he'd shown up. What was occurring in her life when he'd appeared before?

The first time she saw him was after she fell into the well. Then, it was around the time she read from Maggie's book. These were all very different times, but they all revolved around danger. She wished Maggie was there to could confer with her. Maggie would have an explanation; she was certain of that.

She wondered if she should speak to Mitch about it. What would he say if she told him? Would he think she was crazy? She was sure he would. It would be better to hold off and talk to Dennis when they were alone.

She rubbed the chill from her arms. The wind had picked up outside and the house was cooling down. It was time to head upstairs to snuggle under her thick goose down comforter. She would get a good night's sleep and then decide if she would confide in Mitch or not in the morning.

As she flipped off the light switch it dawned on her that the first time she saw the ghost wasn't in her bedroom after the accident. It was while speaking with Mitch on the telephone. In fact, every time the ghost appeared, Mitch had either telephoned, was visiting, or was on his way to visit.

THREE

Tara was lightly dozing off when she heard the unmistakable padding of slippered feet on the wooden landing as they made their way past her bedroom door. Her bedroom was at the top of the first flight of stairs and centered between the guest quarters and the stairwell that led to the third floor. The creaking of the hardly used door at the base of that stairwell signaled to her that whoever was tip toeing around wasn't heading to the kitchen for a snack. There hadn't been enough time passed since she and Mitch were dating for her to forget the sound of his footsteps, which left only one other person; Alana.

Why would she be sneaking upstairs; especially after Tara specifically kept it out of their tour, explaining its disrepair as hazardous? In its days of glory, the third floor of the house was the residence for the servants. Since her grandmother neglected to maintain things for so many years, there was structural damage on the top floor where the leaky roof and broken windows left some of the rooms at the mercy of the elements. She'd declared it off limits to everyone, especially her guests. She boarded the windows and repaired the leaky roof almost immediately upon taking possession of the house, but there were still plenty of hazards for someone maneuvering around, particularly at night. Sliding out of bed she jammed her feet into her slippers, donned her well-worn robe, grabbed a flashlight from the drawer of her night stand and left the warmth of her renovated bedroom to brave the mercilessly fierce night air of the rest of the house. Stopping at the bottom of the narrow stairwell, she listened intently before cautiously making her way to the third floor. Fearful of it being a potential fire hazard in its present condition, she'd disconnected the electricity on the top floor; making the flashlight her only source of visibility. Stepping as lightly as she could, Tara felt as if she was the intruder instead of the other way around.

She wasn't sure why she wanted to keep her presence a secret. This was her house, after all. Even so, somehow, she felt like she shouldn't be there.

She'd ventured onto the third floor three times since moving into the house. She took a tour with her father while awaiting the moving van, and shortly afterward when a repair company estimated the cost to bring it back to its original state of charm and glory. The number set Tara on her heels. She decided that until the main part of the house was finished she'd put the resurrection of the third floor on hold and just make it off limits to everyone for safety's sake. She ventured up there the third time to instruct the workers she hired to do the necessary repairs to the roof, disconnect the electricity and board the windows.

When she reached the top step, a thin beam of light moved near her. She ducked down to avoid being seen. The weak beam from Alana's undersized flashlight continued to comb the dusty great room that must have been the main room for the servants. Leading from this former great room that still harbored energy of time gone by was a long hallway with doorways that opened to smaller rooms that were humble in comparison to the spacious and grand rooms below.

Tara watched with amazed wonder as Alana rummaged through the enormous steamer trunks that were clustered in the center of the cluttered room. She acted intent on leaving disarray and mayhem behind her without a care of what Tara might think when she finally did venture upstairs. What is she looking for? Tara shifted to a more comfortable position. The scent of old dust swirled through the stale air at the disruption of fabric that hadn't been touched for possibly a century or more. She held her finger to her nose as she forced back a sneeze that threatened to burst forth.

Oddly enough Tara had no desire to interrupt her house guest. There was something intriguing about skulking about in the middle of the night watching this strange and beautiful woman rummaging through her dusty old unused rooms looking for heaven knows what. Alana's perfect face glowed in the dim light and cast shadows in multiple directions. It had a surreal mesmerizing effect.

Tara was certain that if her presence was known, Alana would cease her hunt. If she did, would she confess to the purpose of her search? She didn't know her well enough to have that answer, but she guessed she wouldn't. Not only was Mitch's new bride-to-be exceedingly beautiful, but she proved mysterious as well.

Alana's search uncovered a group of portraits. From what Tara was able to make out as the weak beam briefly illuminated them, they could be more of the same that were in the stable loft. If so, the artist was kept quite busy. Tara assumed they were portraits of her ancestors and wondered why her grandmother cared for them so poorly. She vowed to return to go through them more closely and perhaps put them in a friendlier environment for safe keeping. If they were in decent condition she would display them in the great room downstairs or along the hall like she saw in many grand ancestral estates.

"Drat!" Alana's muffled voice mixed with the clanking of metal as a tin type crashed to the ground.

Sensing her secret scavenger was about to abandon her search, Tara took advantage of the commotion and dashed back to her room. As she leaned against her bedroom door she was barely able to hear the padding of Alana's feet as she hurried back to her room above the crashing of her thunderous heart.

This unexpected event had adrenaline coursing through Tara's veins and there was no way she could go back to sleep. She stayed motionless against the door while she waited for her heartbeat to slow down and hearing to come back to normal.

Opening her door just far enough to hear better, she listed for sounds of activity. When she was satisfied no one else was up and wandering the house, Tara grabbed her large flashlight and made her way back up the stairwell to the third floor.

Her curiosity was peaked and she wouldn't be able to sleep until she investigated what the dusty and cluttered third floor could possibly offer a stranger visiting her home. The brilliancy of the beam from her large flashlight was in stark contrast to the faint eerie lighting that Alana's minuscule beam provided.

Standing at the top of the stairwell, she gasped as she took in the chaos that woman created. Of course, this floor was abandoned for a length of time that Tara could only guess at. Even so, it had been a neat kind of cluttered abandonment. What she witnessed now was indescribable chaos. Could it be that Alana thought Tara was so unfamiliar with its condition that she wouldn't notice it was ransacked? Or, perhaps she simply didn't care? Did she find what she was searching for?

The richness and glitter of the thick deep blue velvet adorned with tiny crystals that peeked out of an oversized trunk caught her eye. She lifted the trunk's lid, being careful not to disturb the thick layer of dust to the point where it would fall onto the remarkably well-preserved clothes within. Pulling the heavy gown to its full length, she held it out to admire it. Spotting a full-length mirror in the corner of the room, she wiped its surface with an old curtain that lay on the floor nearby and held the dress against her body.

The nineteenth century ball gown was her size, something she found interesting since she was taller than the average female of that era. Turning slowly from left to right gave her a better visual of how she might look in such a dress. Although the lighting was far more effective than before, she'd left the flashlight propped by the trunk and was now standing in the outer rings of its illumination. As a result, her image had a mysterious, hazy effect.

As she continued to admire the elegant dress of yesteryear, the room's reflection slowly changed. Her surroundings shifted from a dimly lit, dismal and dusty attic-like room to a brilliant, spotless quarterage. Startled, she dropped the gown and turned around only to find that the room was still dark, dreary and deserted.

Closing her eyes, she took a deep breath and braced herself to face the mirror once again. With her eyes still closed, she picked up the gown and rested it against her body. This time prepared for the vision that would follow, she slowly opened her eyes. Straining to view the room through the mirror's reflection, Tara marveled over its beauty. Even though this was clearly the residence of the help, it was still a fine room.

Behind her, the carved and gilded beech wood of the nineteenth century winged back armchair glistened from loving care and attention while the silk and its Beauvais tapestry cover sparkled with freshness. She longed to turn around and find such a chair behind her to relish and sit enveloped in its beauty.

Spotting a marble top commode off in the distance, Tara wondered how she missed its existence. Its finely polished, gilded mahogany was exquisite. The abundance of French influenced nineteenth century furniture brought many questions about her ancestor's to Tara's mind. Clearly their Irish heritage didn't define their taste in décor.

Disappointed when the mirror once again reflected the dimly lit dusty decay of its former splendor, she turned to search for the marble topped commode. Although not all of the furniture she enjoyed in her vision was still in the room, she instinctively knew that if she searched for the commode she'd find it.

Carefully laying the dress over the now faded armchair, she took a moment to lament the chair's loss of its former splendor before picking up her flashlight and directing it to the part of the room where her she remembered the mahogany commode in her vision. She smiled with satisfied delight at the delicate marbled wisps of white and black stone peeking from beneath a pile of precariously stacked boxes.

She pulled at the stack of boxes, hoping the marble wasn't cracked and the wood was in restorable condition. The windows in this room hadn't needed boarding so perhaps the ravaging fingers of the elements hadn't stretched this far into the house.

She was standing back, catching her breath after removing the final box, when she heard a familiar male's whispered voice, "Lucy." Startled, she lost her balance and fell against the cool marble and was only able to catch a glimpse of her resident ghost as he faded into nothingness. Propping against the commode to support her shaky legs, she willed her body to relax and headed back to bed. She would return for the marble top commode and tidy up the place in the daylight. Making a mental note to find a polite way to question Alana about her actions, she crept her way back to her room and immediately fell into bed. She was exhausted.

****

Alana's statuesque poise was in stark contrast to the dark circles under her eyes as she silently nibbled dry rye toast and sipped black coffee. Mitch questioned her apparent mood and was rewarded with a scowl accompanied by a reply of 'nothing's wrong'. Seeing his love like this for the first time was unsettling. He questioned his wisdom in introducing her to Tara. Could it be she figured out Tara had been more to him than just the younger sister of his good friend? If so, it might account for her sullen mood.

Mitch smiled to himself. How could his gorgeous fiancé possibly harbor jealousy over another woman? Grant it, Tara was a beauty in her own right and he could see her rivaling Alana for attention in certain circles, but by no means was she

Alana's superior. She was her equal maybe, but not superior.

Women were an odd lot.

Even though Tara's return to the house from the stable was through the utility room off the kitchen, the cold air that rushed in behind her managed to find its way into the dining room. Mitch shivered in defense. He moved to the doorway of the kitchen and watched her finish stomping the snow off her knee-high boots and then shake her coat free of the pesky white stuff before hanging it up on the hook above the boot rack.

Mitch marveled over how methodically she removed her boots and placed the boots carefully in their designated space on the rack before slipping on her sheepskin slippers with apparent little thought of her actions. It looked well-rehearsed.

Her rosy cheeks accentuated her rich green eyes as she smiled and made her way to the coffee pot for a hearty mug of the aromatic liquid. Caressing the steaming cup, she nodded to Mitch while she slid past him through the door and made her way to her favorite spot at the dining table. Looking at Tara in the morning light, Mitch could easily understand why his fiancé might harbor jealousy toward the woman. Although he would have liked to hang around to see Dennis, he thought it best they leave as soon as possible.

"I thought we'd head out today," Mitch stated as he cleared his throat.

"Why?" Alana and Tara responded simultaneously.

Surprised at his fiancé's reaction, Mitch stuttered, "Well, I noticed that you seemed tired and tense and I thought perhaps we were overdoing things, my love. I've been dragging you all over in my exuberance to show you off." He turned to Tara, "You have your hands full just surviving the winter without having us underfoot."

"Nonsense," Tara countered. She wasn't about to let Alana leave without the mystery of her rummaging excursion on the third floor being resolved first. "Besides, Dennis is coming today and he'll be disappointed if you're gone. I know he's looking forward to meeting Alana."

Tara eyed Alana warily. She knew all too well the reason behind the dark circles under the woman's eyes. She just didn't know the motive behind them. She thought about just bringing things out in the open and mention Alana's late-night wanderings, but decided it might be for the best if she didn't let on to Alana that she was even aware of her midnight ransacking until she found out her reason for it.

Alana watched her fiancé seat himself next to her in silence. After studying him for a brief moment, she reached across the table and caressed his forearm.

"Darling, I'm fine. Really I am," she cooed. "I just didn't sleep well last night. The house is lovely, but it's old and full of noises that I was acutely aware of. An afternoon nap will correct everything. Please, let's not leave on my account." She leaned back and smiled over the rim of her coffee cup. "Besides, I'm eager to meet this Dennis I've heard so much about. If he's anything like his sister, I know I'll like him."

Tara eyed Alana with wary surprise, but said nothing. She had to give the woman credit. She was good.

Mitch was both relieved and confused by her last remark.

"Well, I guess I'm out voted," he said. Standing and stretching in a cat-like manner, he turned to Tara. "Since I'm here... ya got any chores for me ma'am?" he asked with an emphasis on his attempt at a southern drawl.

The two women chuckled.

Mitch may have regretted his statement, but he didn't show it as he listened to Tara's request for assistance with carrying in enough firewood for several of the fireplaces. Tara assumed he was grateful that she only asked him to carry it and not chop it. Fortunately for all concerned, Brandon chopped a considerable supply of firewood to keep himself occupied while awaiting her recovery from their traumatic ordeal at the hands of Dominic.

Alana took the afternoon to rest up. Dennis was expected for dinner and she wanted to be at her best for their introduction, which meant sleeping away those dark circles. She wondered who he was really and why he passed himself off as Lucy's brother. Oddly, Lucy didn't remember her. At first Alana thought she was putting on a show for Mitch, but as time wore on she realized it was true. Alana was warned that one's memory could be affected during the transport through time, but it was usually temporary. Is that what happened to Lucy? It didn't seem possible. She was a strong witch, after all. Her mind shouldn't have been affected at all. Alana's certainly wasn't. But then, Dominic said Lucy suffered memory loss in Shadow Land so perhaps that played a part in what was going on now.

Tara used this time to pull Mitch into the attic to retrieve the marble topped commode. Not a fan of anything older than a decade, Mitch groaned his distaste while he sneezed his way through the dust filled room. He heaved the ornate commode onto his shoulder and carried it down the stairwell as if it was nothing more than a box of feathers. Tara never ceased to admire the brute strength this man possessed and was never happier than now that he possessed it.

The commode was far lovelier than she imagined. She couldn't wait to see it cleaned up and displaying its rich, historic beauty. It fit perfectly beneath the large, antique mirror in the hallway. Standing back with her hands on her hips, she admired it briefly before rushing to the cleaning closet for the necessary supplies in hopes of returning the dry, dusty gilded mahogany to its original rich luster.

Since her inheritance of the estate house, Tara discovered an array of riches in the form of antiques. Much of the furnishings dated back far enough to have been considered an antique when first placed in the house. Surely, they could have commanded a good price at an antique auction and helped in the maintenance of such an unusually grand estate, but then from the funds left by her grandmother there was no need to sell one stick of furniture. There was also no reason for the dilapidated condition of the house. She often questioned her grandmother's reasons for neglecting it.

After standing and admiring her handiwork, she suddenly remembered the portraits in the loft above Sugar. They weren't as safe from the elements as the ones on the third floor. Eager to rescue them, she rushed downstairs and donned her boots and coat, thankful the sun was brilliant enough to make visibility in the loft easy without a flashlight.

The brilliant rays coming through the open door she'd used to jump through during that horrific storm provided better than adequate lighting for a clear view of the portraits. As she slowly poked through the stack of various sized paintings of familiar feeling faces secured in beautiful antique frames resting against the interior wall of the old building's upper floor, she wondered why her grandmother left their family memories at risk of destruction by the elements. She questioned so much of her grandmother's actions. She would move them all back into the house and put them where they wouldn't be at risk by the elements until she could determine what to do with them. It might be fun to investigate the ancestry registries on the internet and discover who was who.

The framing was constructed of mahogany, cherry, or birch. Although making a beautiful outline around the portrait, lifting the larger ones was difficult. She'd need help. She selected the ones she was confident she could manage on her own and set them aside.

She was only a portrait or two away from the end of the stack when she froze in disbelief. There, standing tall behind an attractive woman seated in a beautiful nineteenth century cruelled tapestry winged back chair was her resident ghost. The hairs stood at attention on her neck as she studied the portrait more closely. She recognized the room in the portrait. It was the one she used as her formal sitting room. She was certain the chair was the one she saw in her vision in the mirror the night before.

This was all too eerie.

Taking a closer look at the woman seated in the chair, there was a familiarity about her that reached down into Tara's bones. Who were these people? Why was he haunting her?

She couldn't explain why, but she wasn't ready for others to view this portrait. She needed time to understand what was happening. If Maggie was alive, she'd ask her about it and would have gotten a logical explanation, but Maggie wasn't alive and she was more alone than she cared to be.

A brief thought of Liam passed through her mind before she pushed it away. She hadn't communicated with him since he gave her Maggie's message. He'd spoken of Maggie and said she was well and happy. Knowing that provided some semblance of comfort.

Thinking of Liam brought back memories of everything else that happened. The wounds were still too raw. After all, it happened only a few months ago. The type of healing she required would take much longer than that.

Although she was grateful to Liam for coming to their rescue, there was still so much she didn't understand. Why did a spirit guide have to wait to be called upon before he could help someone who was in perilous need of assistance? Why did Liam allow Dominic and his demon wolves to rip Maggie to shreds? If Liam was sent to guide and protect her, then why didn't he just step in and protect her and the ones she loved? Why? Why? Why? It was all very confusing and still too painful to think about.

She hadn't thought of Liam since he stood before her and she asked him if she could enter the shadows in time. He responded in turn that 'anything is possible if you believe'. Was that true? Would she find Maggie there?

Her life changed so drastically since she moved into this estate and she wasn't altogether happy with the changes. She loved and was bonded to her ancestral home and looked forward to the day when it was finally restored to its rightful beauty, but she was lying if she didn't admit regrets about the loss of innocence moving into it caused. The underworld, other worlds, and the worlds beyond were what she read about in novels or watched on the big screen or DVD. They weren't supposed to be part of her reality.

Picking up a stray burlap bag from the floor, she shook as much dust free as she could and secured it around the portrait of the old ghost with baling twine. The wood's density made the portrait extremely weighty and cumbersome as she tucked it away in the far recesses of the loft floor for safe keeping until she could return with help to retrieve it.

The sound of pacing below alerted her to the hour. She hurriedly gathered what she was able to carry and made her way down the stone stairway that led to the lower level. Carefully positioning her burden on the bottom step, she headed toward the feed room. She might as well feed and care for Sugar while she was there. Hopefully, by the time she went back to the house, Dennis would have arrived.

***

Don't miss out on the rest of Tara's fantastic and fascinating story. Get your copy of THE SEARCH FOR THE CRYSTAL KEY from your favorite bookseller.

Paranormal Romance Books by Eileen Sheehan

Vampire Witch Trilogy
Vampire Witch: Book 1
Vampire Queen: Book 2
Kings & Queens: Book 3

The Vampire, The Handler, and Me
For Love of a Vampire
The Princess and the Vampire King
Dream Love
Dragon Love
Shadow Love ONE
Shadow love TWO
A Vampire's Love
Emergence

a Wolf Affair: Book 1
Wolf Mountain: Book 2

Dark Escape Book 1
The Search for the Crystal Key Book 2

Thrillers by Eileen F. Sheehan
The Tugurlan Chronicles
Vampire Iniquity: Book 1
The Cure: Book 2
Vampires and Werewolves: Book 3

VICKIE
Ghost Love

Historical and Contemporary Romance Books by Ailene Frances
Love Misunderstood
Paper Widow
Love at Wolf Creek

For Love or Money

****

Alternative Romance Books by E. F. Sheehan
Toast with Jelly
The Tragedy of a Lesbian Confused

Eileen Sheehan primarily writes hot, steamy romances (mostly New Adult) with a sexy male and strong female. A few are steamier than others (see their description). The majority of her novels are paranormal, but some are just plain novels about people in love (contemporary or historical with the author name of Ailene Frances). ALL of her stories have a bit of naughtiness, some excitement, a few thrills, and maybe a touch of mystery mixed in with sometimes naughty, sometimes sweet lovin'. She strives to write a novel length that will allow the busy woman to be able to sit down in an evening or two and be taken on a romantic journey without having a week go by before she gets to the end of the story.

An incurable romantic, she has a love affair with at least one of her characters... one book at a time. She hopes the same thing happens to you.

More Information:
Eileen Sheehan started out as a freelance writer for periodical magazines and newspapers. From there, she tried her hand at writing screenplays. Her screenplay, "When East Meets West" was a finalist in the 2001 Independent International Film and Video Festival at Madison Square Gardens, NYC. Finally finding her niche, she lets her imagination loose with new adult/paranormal romance/thrillers (some are steamy and some are tame) with the pen name of Eileen Sheehan. She creates steamy historical romances and plans on writing contemporary romances at some point with the pen name of Ailene Frances. Seeing how far out of the box she could stretch, she crafted an alternative romance with the pen name of E. F. Sheehan and has a few self-help books under her work name of Lena Sheehan.

A Personal Note from Eileen:

Hello all of you paranormal/ romance/ horror/ thriller fans! Thank you for supporting me as an indie author. If you could feel inclined to write a review, or even simply tell a fellow reader that you enjoyed my books I'd be eternally grateful. Reviews are one of the primary things that amazon looks at when referring a book to others, which makes them almost as important as sales. If you want to see more quality writings at a reasonable price, please support my efforts by leaving a review.

Thanks!

Earth Wise Books